The Mysterious Kingdom
of the Arroyo

Saving the World from Chaos

Boualem Bousseloub

Table of Contents

Chapter One:

Encounters in the Arroyo

Blanca, the Mysterious Visitor

It is a mild early Saturday afternoon. Out in the sun, it might quickly feel almost too warm, but under the trees of the arroyo in front of the Aquatic Center, it is pleasant. A soft breeze, like an invisible genie, ensures the air remains cool.

Seated at a table under a tree, Sarah, a young cardiac nurse, reads a recently published magazine with an article on depression. Twenty feet away, reclining against a grassy mound, her son Astor is also reading. He is very absorbed in an illustrated field guide to...rabbits.

It has been barely ten minutes since both started reading when the boy hears someone asking, "What are you reading?"

"You know, Mo...o...om. It's my book on rabbits!" says Astor without looking up.

"I'm not your mom. It's me. Right here. Above you," says the voice again.

Astor looks up and, to his astonishment, sees a rabbit almost his size standing at the top of the mound.

"Hi there," says the rabbit, waving a paw.

"Hi," says Astor, waving back, "Why are you dressed as a rabbit? It's not Halloween yet."

"I *am* a rabbit."

"You are *not*. Rabbits don't talk. I'll ask my mom."

"Go ask your mom. But she can't see me, and she'll only tell you to be quiet."

"Yes, that's what Mom says when she comes back from work with a headache." Astor pouts. The pouting is his way of thinking through an unfamiliar situation. "If my mother can't see you, and I can, doesn't that make me weird? I already feel…"

Before the boy can finish, the rabbit says in a welcoming voice, "No, you are special and I am…a magic rabbit."

"Wow, a magic rabbit! Can you do magic?"

"Yes, some."

"Will you show me? Please!" says Astor, starting to get excited.

To calm Astor down, the rabbit says, "Hold on, let me first take you on a tour of our magical neighborhood."

"Where? I can't go anywhere. My mom…"

"I know," interrupts the rabbit, who feels the child's disappointment. "But I am forgetting my manners. First, let me introduce myself. My name is Blanca. I am a cottontail."

"I know what a cottontail is," answers the boy, his enthusiasm returning. "I have seen some here in the arroyo. They are mysterious. That's why I read about rabbits. Do you live here, too?"

"Yes, I do. Actually, all those rabbits you have seen were me," says Blanca with a smile. "I wanted you to get to know me. That's why any time you came to the arroyo, I showed up."

Astor stands up, stretching his skinny ten-year-old self. He brushes grass and dirt from his favorite well-worn jeans and his blue T-shirt. "Nice to meet you, cottontail Blanca. I'm Astor," says the boy. "This is my name," he adds, pointing a finger to his chest.

Blanca notices the name "Astor" is written vertically on the boy's T-shirt. Each letter, in turn, starts a name horizontally. All around the names are musical notes. She makes a mental point to ask Astor about the horizontal names and the musical symbols later.

"Nice to meet you too, at last," says Blanca.

The boy and the rabbit shake hand and paw.

"How come when you speak, I can hear you, and my mother can't?"

"That's because I am not speaking. I'm mentally communicating with you. You hear my voice in your head. Now, tell your mom you want to go for a walk and ask for her permission." The rabbit grins.

"She will say NO!"

Blanca's voice drops to a whisper. "Please, just ask her anyway."

Astor does. Surprisingly, his mother says yes, without asking where he'll be going.

"What happened?" asks the boy, returning to the rabbit.

"Your mother didn't refuse because she is so engrossed in her reading. She loves you very much and wants to find out all she can about her...condition."

"You mean her depression. I know about it."

"Yes, I mean depression. What parents want is to help their children—"

"You know about depression?" interrupts Astor, his large eyes bright in his face.

"Your mother knows that you will be happier when she learns to manage her depression," says Blanca.

A short moment of silence follows.

"I cast a light spell on your mother," says Blanca.

"Will your spell hurt her? Turn her into a witch or a toad?" asks the boy, alarmed.

"Not at all! She'll remain reading and be sure of your presence here. Anyway, we'll be back before she knows we're gone."

So in the company of his mysterious new friend, Astor crosses from the Aquatic Center to the other side of the street, to the path used by riders from the nearby equestrian center.

Walking side by side, Astor and Blanca go south along the wash. They walk uphill for a while and, at the curve before the road dips under the Pasadena Bridge, they enter the arroyo at the point where riders do.

There are no horses and riders at that moment.

"This is our lookout post," says Blanca, pointing to a tall tree. Its straight trunk seems perfect for a sentry's role.

"How can it be a lookout if nobody's there?" says Astor.

"Watch!" Blanca claps her paws.

A squirrel appears from the other side of the trunk. He moves his eyebrows up and down, bringing a smile to Astor's face, before quickly disappearing up the tree and out of sight.

Blanca and Astor continue past a small pond, which is actually a tiny branch of the arroyo, covered almost entirely in watercress.

Three male mallard ducks with brown chests and iridescent heads swim in the company of three females with drab colors.

"Ducks!" says Astor in an excited voice that sets the birds quacking. They give three quick quacks, then swivel their heads so that for a moment, Astor thinks they're looking right at him. Then they give a single long quack.

"Sentries. They first sounded the alarm but then recognized me and canceled it. There are more sentries. Look over there," says Blanca. She points at two crimson dragonflies whirling around like children playing a game before landing on two separate twigs.

"They are our low-flying…eyes," says Blanca, acknowledging the iridescent insects with a nod. "I told them to keep an eye on your mother. They will immediately advise me by long-range telepathy of anything unusual. You don't have to worry; your mother is in good hands."

"You mean in good eyes," says Astor, thinking of the multifaceted eyes of the dragonflies. He feels good about his mom being under their protection.

Astor and Blanca stop to listen to the water lapping quietly against the rocks. At a distance Astor notices a clump of dried plants and feels sorry for them.

He hears a voice in his head. *Don't be sorry. Their seeds are graciously offered as part of nature's cycle. This winter's rain will sow them downstream.*

Astor remembers it is Blanca communicating with him. *What a cool way to talk to those you like. I'll ask Blanca to teach me,* he tells himself.

As they make their way down the path, Blanca and Astor come to a huge, bent oak tree. From a distance, they can see how the tree's gnarled trunk leans toward the earth, its old tired branches bending to rest on the ground.

As they come closer, Astor notes the tree's limbs create a natural awning over a warm inviting space.

"This is our Open Court of Conventions," says Blanca. "It's where matters of utmost importance to our kingdom are discussed and voted on."

Astor senses a certain energy filling the space, as though the weight of those decisions lingers here. Astor and Blanca pause a moment, giving the feeling the respect it deserves, then cross through the space, coming out the far side.

Suddenly, looming not three feet in front of them, a huge rock covered with vegetation appears. Lichens and mosses make patterns on its surface that remind Astor of what he sees when he looks through his dad's telescope at the surface of the moon.

The rock towers over them, blocking their way.

As many times as Astor had walked along the arroyo with his father, he has never noticed this imposing mass of rock, an island in the middle of the dry creek bed.

Blanca steps to the right of the boulder and whistles. It isn't really a whistle. She just makes a sound like the first time a child tries to whistle. Astor's ears capture an unusual vibration, something he is not familiar with. His keen musician hearing senses more than hears an ultrasonic sound that usually only dogs can hear.

Without warning, a large portal of bronze suddenly appears in front of them.

"Wow," exclaims Astor, fascinated, his eyes growing larger than two saucers.

Two loud creaks then one crack are followed by a soft whoosh.

The portal opens.

Chapter Two:

Inside a Dazzling Castle

A smile blooms on Blanca's face as she points her paw at the portal. "After you."

They step into a magnificent hallway with walls of thick pink marble and a floor of lapis lazuli glowing in a peaceful, liquid-gold light.

"I can't believe my eyes. I must be dreaming," says Astor.

"No, you are not."

"Are you making this up, then?"

"No, I am not."

"How come my father..." The boy stops, sadness flooding his throat.

Blanca touches his arm, and he is able to continue.

"How come my father, who knew everything, never mentioned this...palace?

"Yes, this is a palace, The Palace of the Serene Soul. He did not know about this place. *You* are the first human to enter this magic realm."

"*I am?*" shouts Astor, forgetting the sadness he was just feeling as he thought about his father and how much he misses him.

After a brief hesitation, Astor, followed by Blanca, moves further into the hallway, which seems endless from where Astor and Blanca stand. As they pick up their pace and hurry forward, Astor imagines himself embarking on a voyage of discovery.

The air inside the hallway carries a strange stillness. Astor can feel a sadness matching his own.

The Rainbow Throne

Within a short time, the hallway abruptly turns right, and a huge carved door encrusted with sparkling jewels looms before them. Just as abruptly, the door opens without a sound and rescues them from the melancholy of the hallway.

Astor and Blanca enter a vast room with golden walls and tall windows hung with beautiful, billowing white drapes. A secret breeze blows gently into them.

"This is the Hall of the Rainbow Throne," declares Blanca in a hushed voice, like the one Astor heard his mother use at his father's funeral.

The enormous room is empty except for a strikingly painted throne, which stands at the far end of the hall.

Its vibrant and pulsating palette of colors dazzles the boy, forcing him to blink his eyes several times to adjust his vision.

"Come forward, Blanca, and introduce your guest," says a deep voice.

Astor is surprised because he hadn't noticed anybody sitting on the throne, yet the unexpected voice doesn't startle him. In fact, the soft notes of caring that layer the voice soothe Astor.

"Lord Iridio," says Blanca, bowing deeply. "I present you Astor, the boy I told you about. "Astor," says Blanca grandly, "This is Lord Iridio, Master of the Rainbow and Protector of the Arroyo."

Lord Iridio nods almost imperceptibly at Astor; still the boy feels respect in the gesture.

Astor addresses the extraordinary being with a bow. "Glad to meet you, Lord Iridio."

Astor is surprised by his own polite reaction. Yet he is only behaving in ways his mother, father, and grandmother have tried to teach him. Although he had previously shown only a passing interest in it, the teaching has indeed borne fruit. His family would be proud of him.

Standing before the throne, Astor is completely mesmerized by the being sitting on it.

Lord Iridio looks human, but somehow he is different. His jet-black hair is streaked with electric blue. The skin on his face and hands shines gold, with reflections of pink and copper. More strikingly, and adding to Astor's awe, Lord Iridio is silhouetted by an aura of shimmering light, radiating a rainbow of spectacular colors.

Still in wonderment, Astor now notices the palette has a pattern, a very specific pattern of seven colors, all vibrant and shimmering. He vividly recalls the discussion with his father, mother, and grandmother the message of each color. It takes him time to finally settle his mind on these:

Red displays impatience and readiness for action.
Orange warms the heart for friendship.
Yellow sings the virtue of summer.
Green invites us to the coolness of nature.
Blue speaks of air and sea voyages.
Indigo beckons to reading and thinking.
Violet whispers of life's mystery.

It is a rainbow! Thoughts flood Astor's mind. *How could I have missed that? Is it because I never encountered a rainbow so close before, in a room? Is this one real?*

Lord Iridio stands up.

"He is a very young boy," he says in a voice ringing with surprise. "I expected him older."

"Yes, he is young, but he is also a human being with much love and compassion in his heart. I believe Astor to be an *old* soul."

Astor does not understand what "an old soul" means, since he is only ten years old. Then he remembers something his father told him to do when he did not understand the meaning of some words. "Wait before you ask, and make sure to turn your tongue around your mouth seven times. Yes, seven times!"

Astor heeds his father's advice as he wonders who took the rainbow away from the throne. Astor blinks his eyes and looks again at the throne. A glance assures him it isn't what he thought; nobody took the rainbow away.

Lord Iridio is clad in a garment that one minute fits his body like a shimmering white glove, and the next, floats around him as a royal robe of the most splendid blue and burnished gold.

If that were not enough, a shock of light of various colors flows from between his eyes and radiates from his throat and chest.

Lord Iridio opens his hands, cupped as though he has been holding in them the secret of the kingdom. Instantly, two golden macaws appear, each bearing a beautifully gilded armchair covered in a luxurious green that mirrors the deep color of the laurel trees, those noble features of the arroyo.

"Please take a seat," invites Lord Iridio, his voice sounding both musical and kind.

As soon as Astor and Blanca sit down, three young crows in white bowties come in. Each carries a tray with a crystal goblet.

Light dances on the crystal like a never-ending fireworks display.

The aroma of the beverage entices Astor to bend forward in his seat and pick up his goblet. Realizing he is the only one with a goblet in his hand, he hesitates, feeling awkward.

Lord Iridio smiles, his rainbow colors flashing strong, and Astor experiences great relief.

As the colors of the rainbow swirl around him, Lord Iridio picks up his goblet and proposes a toast. "To our Honored Guest, Astor. May his appearance be a good omen for our kingdom!"

Astor knows the word *omen*. His father told him omens were signs from the spirits, some good, and some alarming.

Astor feels relieved knowing he's a *good* omen.

Seeing that Blanca is now sipping from her goblet, Astor puts the ornate glass to his lips.

The drink tastes heavenly. Astor can't describe it. It tastes like vanilla, and raspberry, with a touch of pomegranate juice, his grandmother and his father's favorite drink, all combined into an awesome beverage.

As Astor takes a small sip, his palate tingles.

Blanca notices the smile on Astor's lips. "This is nectar, Lord Iridio's favorite beverage. Our master brewer distills it, in accordance with an ancient recipe, from carefully selected fruit, flower petals, and pollen."

Astor waits for Blanca to finish her explanation and drains his goblet. To his amazement, the goblet immediately refills itself. He begins to take another sip and hears Blanca telling him that, as long as he holds the goblet, it will refill itself.

Reluctantly, Astor puts his goblet down on the tray.

❧

Unannounced, a mouse with a white apron and a powder-blue bonnet scurries into the throne room.

Astor's eyes grow wide as the mouse, whose fur is a fanciful mauvish-pink, bows to the guests before murmuring in Lord Iridio's ear.

The rainbow surrounding the throne begins to pale and the flow of light from Lord Iridio's throat starts to recede. The radiance of his being, which earlier had so dazzled Astor with its power, dims, as though the life force that runs through him is in grave danger of disappearing altogether. The Lord of the Rainbow winces as he speaks. "Would you please excuse me? There is an urgent matter I must attend to."

Looking directly at Astor, Lord Iridio nods. Astor senses a lingering sadness in Lord Iridio. "We will meet again soon, Astor. The signs all portend the importance of your presence here."

Lord Iridio sits back upon his throne and, where there was light and color, only shadow remains.

Blanca curtsies, and Astor bows as they back away from the throne.

❧

The massive oak door silently swings shut, its sparkling jewels now subdued into a cheerless pallor. In the hallway, shadows gather along the marble walls, and their rich pink hue sinks into a dull red. The magnificent lapis lazuli floor looks lifeless.

Astor can taste nectar lingering in his mouth, a sweet memory coming after the sadness they felt in Lord Iridio.

Despite the grave tone of their meeting with Lord Iridio cut short by the mouse's appearance, Astor can't help but ask, "What was that pink mouse? I have seen many gray, brown, and white mice, but never pink. Is she painted?"

"That was Miss Rosette, the head nurse of the palace. No, she is not painted. She is a rare mutation."

"You mean like the flamingos that turn red-pink because of their diet?"

"Not really, something more complex and permanent."

Delighted by the earnest knowledge of her protégé, Blanca smiles. *He will be perfect for the lab.*

Where Knowledge Is Always Welcome

Outside the Hall of the Rainbow Throne, Blanca and Astor have gone a short distance, the way they had come before, when casually Blanca says, "Lord Iridio has welcomed you into the kingdom; now it's time you meet Professor Hoot-Hooty, our Seeker of Knowledge. He is also entrusted with the only copy of the Prophecy of Fire still in existence in its original flame. It has taken him several years to master its Oracle of Inscrutability."

At that moment another hallway, which had been invisible earlier, appears. They go several steps before reaching a green door. Blanca says, "This is the Laboratory of the Perpetual Quest for Knowledge."

Above the door, in exquisite calligraphy, a sign reads:

Enter with knowledge,
Subconscious may it be.
We welcome every hint of
What only you can see.

Before they have a chance to knock, the door opens and they enter an immense room. *Everything is oversized in this palace,* thinks Astor.

The large rectangle of a room is bursting with equipment of various sizes and shapes.

Huge glass containers, like giant fish tanks, hold multicolored solutions. In one of them a thick red liquid lazily swirls around, reminding Astor of Jupiter's Great Red Spot.

Puffs of steam escape from bubbling liquids in tall vials.

Astor recognizes an alembic, an ancient distillation device made up of two containers connected by a glass tube. He recognizes it from an intriguing picture his father had once shown him. In his mind's eye he sees the alembic being used centuries ago by inquisitive individuals called…what were they called? He makes an effort to remember but can't.

Alchemists, says a voice in his head—Blanca's voice.

"Ah yes, al-che-mists," Astor repeats, splitting the word into three syllables; his own way to memorize it.

He smiles and nods thank you.

The alchemists wanted to turn lead into gold, and used the alembic as part of their experiments. *It was an interesting idea,* thinks Astor, *but for myself, I prefer turning dreams into music and music into hope with my violin.*

"Come closer."

The engaging voice of a public lecturer interrupts Astor's thoughts. When Astor refocuses his attention, an owl the size of an adult human flaps a brown wing of greeting. He is working at a machine facing the door.

The owl has enormous eyes and wears equally enormous, square glasses, which move from side to side, giving him the look of two people in one body.

His beak is not the crooked and pointed one typical of his species; it is straight and slightly rounded at the end.

That makes him less scary.

The owl waves Blanca and Astor to two chairs in front of the machine.

Blanca does the introductions. "Professor Hoot-Hooty, this is Astor, the friend I told you about."

"Oh yes! Welcome, young man," says the professor.

"Thank you, Professor. Pleased to meet you, too." Astor smiles in greeting.

For a few minutes, they talk about Astor's trip through the arroyo, his meeting with Lord Iridio, the weather and the beauty of the arroyo.

Rather nonchalantly, the professor says, "With your permission, I would like to conduct a test on you."

Astor is familiar with tests. Since the car crash that killed his father, his mother has been through so many doctors, labs, exams, and tests for her depression. Sometimes he hears her speak about them in phone calls to family and friends. He feels he had gone through them; they have become his tests as well.

Professor Hoot-Hooty's request piques Astor's curiosity. *One more test, conducted by this unusual professor, won't hurt,* he thinks.

"Sure, if we have time," responds Astor.

"Yes, we do have time," confirms Blanca.

A squirrel the size of a greyhound appears carrying in his arms a soft, shining device that he skillfully dusts off with his very abundant tail. *There's no need to dust it. It's shiny enough,* thinks Astor.

When the squirrel positions it on Astor's head, the device turns out to be a helmet.

It has no wires, just two funny-looking antennae that could have been put in by a mischievous troll playing a trick on Professor Hoot-Hooty.

At first, the helmet appears bigger than Astor's head but, coming to life, it molds itself to fit his skull.

Astor doesn't have time to be scared or even surprised. Immediately a warmth similar to that of his mother's hugs engulfs him. *It is a friendly helmet with a warm personality,* thinks Astor. Liking it he decides to trust it.

Two owlets, the same size as Astor—and maybe even his age— come to stand next to Professor Hoot-Hooty.

They are both wearing white lab coats that fit them perfectly.

"Astor, these are my twin assistants, Hooty-Tooty and Tooty-Hooty," says the professor. With his right wing extended, the professor points to the two visitors. "Our Honored Guest, Astor, and our dear friend, Blanca!"

Then, without further discussion, the professor asks Astor, "Ready?"

"Ready," confirms the boy.

The professor turns on the machine, and the test begins.

What follows for Astor is a wild assortment of sensations: a tingling, pleasant warmth swirls through his head and flows into the rest of his body until his fingers and toes feel like singing.

Then he hears music.

"What does this music make you think of?"

"Singing angels," says Astor.

"When you listen to the music, what color do you see?"

"Green," says Astor, feeling the warmth expand in his chest.

"What color do you see now?"

"Blue."

The warmth has moved to Astor's throat.

"How do your hands feel?"

"Very warm."

"What's in your heart?"

"Compassion."

"What color is your soul?"

"Pure white," responds Astor without hesitation, startling himself.

He does not know why he said that. The answer seems to have come from somewhere deep inside him or even beyond him. The soul is something that grownups talk about, something he has never seen, nor has he ever thought about the soul having a color. Now, he knows the color of his own soul? How is that possible?

That is puzzling. Actually, Astor is amazed by all his responses.

A salvo of applause and hooting brings Astor back to the reality of the lab.

"Congratulations. You passed the test!!! You are indeed a healer!"

Astor is intrigued by the test and its results that seems to delight Professor Hoot-Hooty and his team.

"It's time to go," says Blanca to Astor.

"Thank you, Professor Hoot-Hooty, and twin owlets," Blanca says to the crew.

Astor waves, and they both depart.

∾

Once they are back in the hallway outside the lab, Blanca decides it is the right time to ask about Astor's T-shirt.

"May I see your name on the T-shirt?"

Astor nods and straightens himself up.

Stacked vertically, in large block letters starting on the front of the T-shirt near his collarbone and ending just below his ribcage is the name ASTOR.

Horizontally are five other names, which Blanca reads out loud.

"**A**dam, Adolphe-Charles".

"**S**ousa, John Philip."

"Known as 'The March King,'" interrupts Astor.

"**T**aieb, Walter,"

"**O**rff, Carl,"

"**R**avel, Maurice."

"They are musicians, also com...comp..." Astor stops. Finally he adds, "Music writers."

"You mean composers," offers Blanca.

"Yes, com-po-sers, from different parts of the world. It's my *own* world," Astor says cheerfully.

"I only know Ravel and his wonderful *Bolero*," replies Blanca with an apologetic smile.

"You do?" beams Astor. "*Bolero* is one of my favorite pieces." Pleased by Blanca's musical knowledge, Astor claps his hands and inhales a breath of delight. "Adam is the French composer of the ballet *Giselle*. It's my mother's favorite.

My father said it's because, when they saw the show, the main dancer was Nureyev. My mother loves Nureyev."

He stops to catch his breath.

"Taieb is a French musician I discovered on the Internet. With the assistance of another musician, he composed *The Alchemist's Symphony*, a piece I adore.

"Orff is from Germany, where he composed *Music for Children*. I believe it's a teaching method too."

As Astor names the composers, he stops after each one, counting them on his fingers.

"My father named me Astor," volunteers the boy, "because he wanted my name to be easier to pronounce than his own name, Archimedes, or my grandmother's name, Lukky...thea, no, Leu-ko-thea." Astor continues, "My name means *hawk*. He wanted it not to be just easy to say, but also be a name that provides the powers of being *alert and successful*, like a hawk. My father believed in the magic of words and names."

Blanca and Astor return to the grassy area near the Aquatic Center where they had left Astor's mother.

When they arrive, Astor notices that his mother is still under Blanca's spell, reading her magazine.

"When will I see you again?" asks Astor.

"Soon. Your mother will be bringing you back here."

They hug each other good-bye, then Blanca waves her paw at Astor's mother.

At the moment Blanca disappears, Astor's mother looks up at her son and exclaims, "Here you are! I guess it's time to go home. We will come back next weekend."

Grandma's Visit

The following Friday afternoon, when he returns from school, Astor finds his grandmother at the house.

"Grandma Thea!" he shouts, dropping his heavy school pack without closing the door and running into her open arms.

"Astor, the iris of my eyes," she says, picking him up for a kiss on both cheeks.

Grandma Thea has a big task: assisting Astor's mother during her recent depression.

"I came because your mom is going straight from work to a lecture on depression tonight at a nearby library," she says in her Greek-accented English.

His paternal grandmother has come every month for the last six months to spend a week at a time with them. In addition, she also comes when she is needed, like today, to give Astor's mother a hand by caring for him when his mother has lectures or workshops to attend. Finally, she helps when Astor's mother works a weekend shift.

In no time, Thea is in the kitchen and the fragrance of moussaka is wafting into the living room where Astor, sprawled out on the floor, is doing his homework. Thea was able to perform this culinary achievement so swiftly because she came with most of the ingredients already prepared

After dinner, Astor and his grandma enjoy their shared pleasure in music. They sit on the sofa for over an hour together, listening to an album of Greek music that includes the lively *sirtos* that Thea had danced to as a young girl in Greece.

Chapter Three:

The Return to the Arroyo

The next morning, Saturday, Astor's mother is in a great mood. Usually after a workweek, she is very tired and sometimes depressed. The episodes of depression started shortly after her husband Archimedes died in the car crash. Fortunately, the episodes never last more than a few hours.

"Would you like to go to down to the arroyo?" she asks Astor.

"Sure, Mom!"

That surprises her since she expected some resistance from her son.

"I'll fix a picnic lunch to take for us."

And for Blanca, Astor wants to add but refrains.

Astor's mother looks younger with her hair neatly pulled back into a ponytail, her features relaxed, and her eyes twinkling with some inner light.

Astor feels warmth emanating from her. He looks at his mom, perplexed.

She hesitates for a short moment before saying, "Last night's lecture opened my eyes and filled me with optimism. The presenter, a doctor, was remarkable. She knew her complex topic so well that she made it simple to understand."

She stops, remembering some of the moments at the lecture the night before. "I had so many questions when I arrived and left with a lot of answers."

When they arrive at the arroyo, Sarah is pleased to find that the table they used the week before is available. So is Astor's favorite grassy mound.

She checks her watch. "It's ten past ten. We will have lunch at one-thirty unless you get hungry earlier." Then she sits down to read a medical journal.

"Fine!" answers Astor. He looks around for his friend Blanca.

He has barely finished going through a thirsty feeling of expectation when Blanca appears as a rabbit first and immediately morphs into a lovely twelve-year-old girl.

"Wow! You are pretty as a cottontail, but you are prettier as a girl," says Astor.

Blanca blushes briefly. Her dress is lovely. It seems that a seamstress took a bucolic painting of the arroyo and sewed it into a dress.

"Hello, Astor."

"Hello, Blanca."

Speaking at the same time, they grin, laugh and hug like longtime friends.

"Time for us to go," says Blanca.

That's all Astor needs to hear.

And they are on their way, faster than the first time because Astor has relived their earlier trek many times in his mind. He remembers every detail along the path leading to The Palace of the Serene Soul.

The Council of Overflowing Kindness

Blanca takes him straight to the Open Court of Conventions, where several beings sit speaking in low voices. Their murmurs have a somber undertone that alerts Astor.

They are seated around an oddly shaped table, like an oval from which an angry giant has taken a bite. The chairs on that bitten-off side are vacant; that's where Blanca takes Astor. The whole group stands up when the two enter.

Astor doesn't know the group has been assembling for a week or that their meeting is critical to the survival of the world.

Blanca's arrival with Astor serves not only as a relief but as a welcome ray of hope. Astor doesn't understand what's going on but decides to trust his friend Blanca.

She nods, saying, "Allow me to introduce Astor. I am sure by now all of you know he passed the test of Professor Hoot-Hooty."

"Yes," they answer in one voice.

"I'll introduce the members of the Council of Overflowing Kindness," says Blanca to Astor.

Turning to the council members, she says, "When you hear your name, dear councilor, kindly raise your hand, paw, wing, or antenna in acknowledgment."

She starts in a firm voice.

"Talkie-Mockie."

A mockingbird in his gray-and-white suit raises his left wing and tips the black hat tilted over his left eye. "Also known as Talmock, he likes to sing—sometimes off key when he wants one of us to complain."

"If they complain, that means they are listening," Talmock winks at Astor.

I hope to be friends with Talmock; sharing music with him will be a pleasure, thinks Astor.

"Toady-dy."

A croaker of indefinite color and of equally indefinite age raises a massive right limb.

"Welcome-come, Sir Astor-tor," he croaks.

The echo in the toad's throat fascinates Astor. He's also surprised that the councilor called him "Sir." That makes him think of Sir Lancelot, one of his beloved historical characters.

"Señora Tortuga."

A tortoise with an intricately patterned quilt of a shell slowly raises a foot withered by time. "Señora Tortuga was born about thirty years after the San Gabriel Mission was built in 1771. She remembers when the arroyo was pristine and wild, when Native Americans often visited it. Take note that she does *not* like iceberg lettuce, but her daughter Miss Tortuguita, not present at the moment, does. Also unlike her mother, Miss Tortuguita adores wearing makeup and mascara, especially green mascara."

Astor can see no makeup on Señora Tortuga.

"Mantra."

A slender, green praying mantis moves an arm seemingly long enough to reach any corner of the Open Court of Conventions. It startles Astor, who is reassured by Mantra.

"Have no fear, Honored Guest. I only feed on voracious mosquitoes and unworthy husbands."

Feeling safe, Astor bows in her direction.

"Crickety-Crick."

A trim brown cricket, his head topped with a tam-o'-shanter, raises a cane. "Near the arroyo, he lost a leg to a nasty kid who wanted to dismember him just for fun. With the serrated back of his free leg he cut that kid's thumb, ensuring his instant release. Also known as Cri-Cri, he is a direct descendant of Earl Tamani, Protector of the Cricket Hall of Fame."

Astor cannot not remember such a character since cricket is not a sport of his childhood.

"Miss Mariposa."

A magnificent blue, black, and orange wing is raised in an elegant flutter. The butterfly's beauty stuns Astor, who, beside Lord Iridio's, has never seen such a display of colors.

"I am Countessa Marpesa Iole de Costa Rica, "says Miss Mariposa introducing herself rhythmically. "I was captured and brought in for the enjoyment of a butterfly collector; my release was a mistake by my captor's son."

"I like your colors," says Astor.

"Thank you. I like you too."

She unfolds a long and delicate proboscis and waves it gracefully until she touches Astor's cheek. It is as soft as his mother's silk blouse.

"Newtia."

A dull olive-green salamander with small reddish dots slowly raises a front leg. "Along with Professor Hoot-Hooty, Newtia is our other scientist who specializes in remedies, elixirs, and love potions and serve as Special Advisors to Lord Iridio," says a reverential Blanca.

Astor recognizes the word *elixir* as a substance used by the alchemists and wonders if Newtia is one of them.

Yet, for some mysterious reason, Astor feels uncomfortable around the scientist, his stomach tightening into a fist.

At that moment, a picture of a man talking to a woman with a dog on a leash flashes briefly by Astor's eyes, too briefly for him to make sense out of it. Astor just shrugs it off.

The Shocking News

Having finished introducing the council members, Blanca announces, "We have only a short time before Astor's mother starts looking for her son, finds him missing, and calls the police."

"Sir Astor," Señora Tortuga begins at once, "you have been brought—excuse my bad manners—*invited* here because we face a very serious…a critical situation. The council has discussed the matter for days and…we all agree that you need to be made aware of it…before we can look together for a solution." Señora Tortuga's voice is shaky, her speech jerky, and her eyes teary. Astor can see that the venerable tortoise is very upset, but he has no clue about its cause.

She takes a deep breath and, in a voice one pitch below the previous one, says, "Our beloved Lady Irena, Mistress of Singing Waters, is gravely ill. She has been ill for four months now. All of Professor Hoot-Hooty and Newtia's attempts at healing her have been unsuccessful. Both of them have called upon their vast knowledge and extensive experience, and we have put all our resources at their complete disposal. Yet to our dismay, Lady Irena's health continues to deteriorate."

She sighs and pauses to calm herself down, but she is unable to continue.

Mantra takes over. "Lord Iridio, Lady Irena's husband, is so distressed that the rainbow, of which he is in charge, rarely appears anymore. When it does, the rainbow has fading colors."

Immediately that conjures up for Astor Lord Iridio's irregularly flashing and dimming colors during their earlier encounter.

"Lady Irena is also the Guardian of World Peace. Her death would create havoc on Earth. This is an awful thought that we can't entertain without fright. We won't accept the idea that our beautiful world might come to an end very soon."

Raising her voice, she repeats with a cry, *"Her death would create havoc on Earth."*

All the members of the Council of Overflowing Kindness echo Mantra's cry.

At this point Astor feels the individual pain of the members of the Council and understands the urgency of the situation. Having met Lord Iridio but not Lady Irena, Astor thinks to himself, *she must be a kind lady to be so loved.*

"Can you imagine the world going into chaos?" asks Cri-Cri. "Since I lost a leg, it's impossible for me to simply jump from one blade of grass to another as I used to in my childhood. Playing hopscotch with my cane is now my best exercise."

"You are funny. I like you," says Astor, imagining Cri-Cri at his game.

"I like you too, kiddo," answers Cri-Cri. "I'll take you along some day to play hopscotch with a cane, without losing your...tam-o'-shanter. It takes some practicing, you'll find out."

There is a brief pause before Cri-Cri continues. "Could you imagine our council members, friends for so many years, forced to fight each other to survive?

Could you imagine your family torn apart in a world where fire rains from the sky and sinkholes open in the ground?"

He pauses again, choking up.

"Can you imagine the world going into chaos?" continues Talmock. "Chaos... no more music, and...I, Talmock, the greatest singer of all times, would not be able to perform!"

As if on stage, Talmock puffs up his chest, jumps on the table, and begins parading around, singing a beautiful medley of music and sounds. His one-minute rendition of the world-famous "Imagine" by John Lennon is simply brilliant.

All the councilors applaud Talmock. They are grateful for the musical interlude that has taken their minds away from the terrifying situation they are facing.

"Thank you, Talmock...Let us go back to our...*prob...lem*," says Señora Tortuga with a sigh.

"Hold on! Did you say chaos?" asks Astor.

"Yes!" yell Talmock and Cri-Cri together.

"Chaos, that is how it will certainly start," offers Miss Mariposa.

"Chaos! It means '*the Gaping Void*,'" gasps Astor. "My father told me about this Greek word for the emptiness from which everything originated. If we fall back into the void there will be *no way* for us to return."

Miss Mariposa steps in. "Before we sink into what the ancient Greeks thought of as chaos, society will disintegrate into what we today understand as chaos: a state of utter confusion, where no one respects anyone else, much less respects the law. Mayhem will reign in large cities, forcing people to hide in their own homes, quaking in fear."

"What a horrible picture you just painted for us," says Mantra.

A shiver goes around the table.

"What can you do to prevent that?" asks an alarmed Astor.

"What can *we* do, all together?" corrects Miss Mariposa.

"As Señora Tortuga implied earlier, you've been invited here because we need *your* help. "

"What can I do? I am just a kid with...with a lot of...problems. I am often awkward, distracted, and on my own. How can *I* help?" says Astor, holding his empty palms in front of him, truly sorry.

"No, you're not just a kid with problems. You are much more than that!"

Speaking slowly, Miss Mariposa emphasizes each word because she wants her statement to sink into Astor's mind. She knows it has to become his own belief leading to his own action plan.

The tone of her voice causes Astor to look directly into her eyes.

"You and all children your age are special. You just need to search inside yourself and discover your own talent," says Miss Mariposa solemnly.

Astor hears without understanding.

Seeing the puzzled look on his face, Señora Tortuga regains some control over her sighing and explains. "The ancient Oracle of Inscrutability nestled in the flames of the Prophecy of Fire has foretold that Lady Irena would be struck by a life-endangering illness, and that only a being with a pure soul will be able to heal her."

Astor alternates between frowning, making faces, and pursing his lips—his ways of trying to make sense out of this confusing situation. He understand the words but wonders what they have to do with him.

The council realizes that Astor is struggling to understand. They all wait in silence, hoping for some mysterious intercession from the council's collective wisdom.

Suddenly the frowning, the face-making, and the lip-pursing stop. Astor's face lights up like the evening sky over the Rose Bowl on the Fourth of July, as he remembers Professor Hoot-Hooty's puzzling question: "What color is your soul?"

Then he remembers his strange response—pure white—an answer that triggered a salvo of applause and a strong "Congratulations," from Professor Hoot-Hooty himself. The professor had concluded his remarks by saying, "You are indeed a healer."

Healer! Healer! Healer! The word echoes in Astor's mind and, by some magic, it all becomes clear. "Do you mean you expect *me* to heal Lady Irena?" asks Astor.

"Yes, yes, yes, a thousand times yes," the distinguished members of the Council of Overflowing Kindness clamor in unison, as if moved by the hoped-for intercession.

In his excitement, Talkie-Mockie jumps onto the table, immediately followed by Crickety-Crick. They improvise a duet in which Talmock sings one of his creations while Cri-Cri performs a fast and dizzying tap dance. The lithe cricket jumps, shuffles, turns, and twists, keeping the tempo with his twirling cane. All the while the cricket's tam-o'-shanter, obviously possessed by a boomerang genie, returns to Cri-Cri's head whether the dancer propels it forward, backward, or upward.

The show is so mesmerizing that the council members forget they are watching a one-legged performer.

The applause reverberates through the Open Court of Conventions, and all present settle into a great silence of peaceful satisfaction and rising hope.

All bask in an omen of future good fortune.

The Cryptic Message

Finally breaking the silence, Toady-dy, with great dignity and conviction, addresses Astor.

"Sir Astor-tor, you are-are our only chance-ance."

Just as he finishes saying that, the toad starts jumping up and down in a rhythmic pattern: two jumps followed by three jumps, then a pause.

The pattern repeats.

The other members of the council go silent again.

Around the table, this silence is thick, palpable.

"Toady-dy is going into a trance," explains Blanca to Astor.

Immediately a black rat enters the room pulling a red cart. The rat is wearing a red cap and boots, and he has yellow gloves on his forepaws.

In the cart, which is decorated around its edges with blue flashing lights, rides a tortoise with a flamboyant shell. She had been alerted by a message from Blanca.

Is this tortoise trying to emulate Lord Iridio with such a colorful shell? muses Astor.

"This is Miss Tortuguita, daughter of Señora Tortuga. She is very young, only seventy-five years of age," says Blanca.

Astor can see that Miss Tortuguita is indeed a young and elegant tortoise. She wears an abundance of make-up: green mascara on her eyelashes, hot-pink lipstick on her beak, and light mauve blusher on her cheeks. She also carries a mirror to aid with her constant grooming.

Miss Tortuguita knows why she was summoned by special dispatch. It has happened over a hundred times, since she is the only one who, through her special gift, can interpret riddles. And the kingdom in the arroyo is filled with mysteries and riddles.

She takes a seat and, on an invisible cue, Toady-dy stops jumping and starts shaking so strongly that his massive right limb flops around wildly.

Tensing up, Astor can't help fearing for Toady-dy's health. Blanca comes to his rescue by touching his arm and saying, "Don't worry; no harm will come to Toady-dy. That's his usual way." Astor's tension evaporates.

In a voice coming from the center of the trance, Toady-dy makes a sound that holds no resemblance to a croak. Almost human, it has a musical quality, making Astor perk up his ears.

He chants:

Ho het sabement
Het sabement,
On verto vapement
Dore mi fa na
Curare I-re-na.

"Master Toady-dy, I am now here to receive your riddle. Please repeat it," says Miss Tortuguita in a soft and respectful voice.

Toady-dy starts the riddle anew.

Miss Tortuguita stares into her mirror and turns her left foot, holding the mirror sideways like a badminton racket.

Then she moves it from side to side, as though to scoop up frolicking butterflies, but there are neither butterflies nor bees in the Council Chamber.

Toady-dy chants his riddle three times, pausing between the first and the second repetition, breathing deeply.

Each time he speaks, Miss Tortuguita, her eyes closed, repeats her movement.

Toady-dy stops shaking, takes three long breaths, and returns to this moment.

Once Toady-dy completes his incantation, Miss Tortuguita opens her eyes, blinks several times, and takes in a long breath. She exhales slowly. Her deep concentration has kept her breathing very shallow, as when running.

Miss Tortuguita looks intently into her mirror and starts refreshing the mascara on her eyelashes. The Council of Overflowing Kindness erupts in applause, cheers, and shouts of joy.

Astor looks astonished.

"Applying mascara to her eyelashes is Miss Tortuguita's way of announcing that the riddle has been solved," explains Blanca.

Miss Tortuguita's eyelashes, now a thick blue-green, flutter mischievously. She turns the mirror to face her audience. For a brief moment, her face appears in it, flashing a sunny smile.

Lo and behold! Written by an invisible hand, the translation appears on the mirror.

A sharp inhalation of breath by the members of the council fills the room. They regain a silent and noble poise befitting their positions and wait for Miss Tortuguita to interpret the riddle.

Astor remains immobile, apparently unmoved by the display, as if he doesn't understand or care. Only Blanca knows that he is registering every detail of the unfolding events.

He is nonetheless startled when Miss Tortuguita's melodious voice addresses him directly. "Would our Honored Guest, Astor, and Miss Blanca like to hear the results?"

She does not wait for an answer. "Here is your message," says Miss Tortuguita, reading from the mirror:

Oh, the basement!
The basement that is
Not over the pavement
Dore mifa-na,
To heal Irena.

"What's that mean?" responds a skittish Talmock.

"It's almost as mis-clear, I mean as unclear, as before," echoes Cri-Cri, pounding his cane on the floor.

Every time Miss Tortuguita is called upon to interpret a riddle or a puzzle, the pair of *compadres*, Talmock and Cri-cri, go through the same routine, gently making fun of the situation by turning it into a comedy or a drama, depending on their inspiration of the moment.

"Let's see what it means," says Señora Tortuga, confident that her daughter has succeeded since she has been helping with interpretations from the beginning.

"*We must start with the basement.* That is simple in itself," says Señora Tortuga. She nods several times to confirm her words. "The next phrase, '*...that is not over the pavement,*' may need some deciphering. Is the castle basement paved?"

"I've never been there," says Mantra, "but a palace custodian told me a while ago that part of it is."

"That's your answer!" says Miss Mariposa. "Whatever we are looking for will be under the unpaved area."

"Thank you for this great teamwork," says Blanca. "Astor and I will go down to the basement and find this secret door, now unlocked, thanks to Miss Tortuguita's interpretation. Talmock and Cri-Cri will accompany us."

Chapter Four:

In Search of the Proper Instrument

The Test

Blanca and Astor head to the basement, escorted by Talmock and Cri-Cri. They all carry torches picked up from sconces on the walls.

Although very fond of the duo, Astor finds it frustrating to have them around for anything quiet and serious. Talmock and Cri-Cri are arguing, laughing, and waving around the torches, creating a light show on the thick, damp basement walls.

Then as the boisterous duo bump into one another in their exuberant jostling, the light from their torches floods a dark corner of the basement, revealing the unpaved area.

"There!" they both yell, pointing to the corner.

At once they begin arguing. "I saw it first," sings Talmock, parading around with chest puffed out.

"You did not!" counters Cri-Cri. "Your eyes are no good in the dark."

"What do you know about my eyes? Don't forget I'm related to the keen-eyed eagle."

"Ah, ah, ah!" laughs Cri-Cri, twirling around on his cane like a dervish. "If *you* are related to the eagle, *I* am related to the dinosaur!"

"You, related to dinosaurs? Maybe to a horsefly, lost in the dirty mane of a dead donkey!" retorts Talmock.

"Be quiet and behave for a moment!" scolds Blanca. "If not, off you go!" she adds pointing a finger to the hallway leading back to the Council Chamber.

Blanca is a genuinely good-natured person, who enjoys their shows, laughs at all of their jokes. She is Cri-Cri and Talmock's best audience and friend, but she also knows when to be firm with them.

Cri-Cri and Talmock's antics come to an instant halt.

Then, as they all walk toward the dark corner, Blanca's right foot bumps into a cobblestone set in the dirt slightly higher than the others. As she does, a loud and sudden bang shatters the short-lived silence.

An ornate metal box springs up in the corner. It is an indistinct, gray-brown color.

Everybody stops.

While the others quickly regain their composure, Astor remains rigidly in place, eyes wide open.

Nobody knows that Astor is terrified of the gray-brown color combination. With great effort, his voice barely a whisper, Astor tells them, "I am allergic to these colors." This color combination is alarmingly unhealthy to Astor. At times, it triggers a state of confusion that leads into a loud and painfully steady pounding in his skull. Even music can become his enemy. Ultimately all that may descend into a sleepy state frighteningly close to a coma.

Light from the torches casts dancing shadows on the box's metal surface, making its colors turn grayer and browner.

This is not good, thinks Astor.

Then he turns his mind to the reason they came to the castle basement—*saving Lady Irena and the world from chaos.*

This steels his resolve.

Astor understands he needs to access his personal weapon against the fear, which grows even stronger when an image of Newtia suddenly springs into his mind. Astor has no idea why the image of the salamander appears at that moment.

He doesn't have time to explore the reason because his personal weapon needs to be used within a minute and half of seeing that dreaded color combination. About thirty seconds have already passed, and terror is starting to take hold of him. Oddly, this new mental image of Newtia begins to take on a muddied gray-brown hue.

Most distressingly yet, Astor feels the power of his fear gather in the image of Newtia.

How can I let that happen...to all these good people who are counting on me? he thinks.

He knows he has only seconds to act. Legs apart, Astor plants himself in the ground as firmly as he can to resist the evil power.

Eyes focused on the terrifying colors, which are getting more terrifying every second in the flickering torchlight, Astor starts humming an ancient Greek song. Slowly, the reassuring vision of a powerful Hercules brandishing his massive club emerges amid the colors.

That vision is Astor's secret weapon against his fear.

Hercules is Astor's favorite ancient Greek because he was part man and part deity and had to perform twelve incredible works to rid the world of evil. Like many young boys and girls, Astor wants to help make the world a better place for all beings, human, animal, and vegetal.

By now, Astor is already partly kneeling, one knee on the ground.

The terror is unrelenting.

I can't...let these people down. I can't...I can't, Astor tells himself holding back tears.

Conjuring the image of his hero, he holds it in his mind.

A strong sensation makes itself known in the other knee. Astor knows it has become the next target of his fear.

In a truly Herculean effort, marked by profuse sweating and intense shaking of his arms, he refuses to let the second knee touch the basement floor.

He does not want to experience the kind of music his father called...

What is the word?

He cannot not remember.

Yet the memory of his father provides him some warmth. He thinks the word starts with *cac. Caca.* No, Father did not use that word. *Caco...oh yes! Cacophonic, harsh sounding!* he screams inside himself.

Astor keeps his inner vision on Hercules until, in his mind, he becomes the Greek hero.

First, he controls the shaking of his arms, then the weakness in his knees.

Finally, he stands up, determined and ready for what might come next. He is ready, his mind intent and his body poised for action.

He doesn't know he is in for the adventure of his life!

All this time, Blanca, Cri-Cri, and Talmock have been silent, unaware that Astor is fighting his fear; they sense nonetheless that something decisive is going on.

They wait in total silence, powerless witnesses to Astor's struggle.

Astor blinks his eyes several times and smiles calmly.

He knows he has once more defeated fear, his personal demon.

Talmock and Cri-cri break out in applause, songs, dances, cries, and yells.

Relieved, Blanca joins in.

Astor doesn't have time to savor his victory, or even thank his friends for their quiet support.

He moves toward the safe, without any idea how to open it. Thoughts flood his mind. *What if it holds the secret to Lady's Irena's recovery? Will he know what to do with it?*

As Astor, confused yet hopeful, approaches the safe, the ornate metal box suddenly changes into a serene pale blue and opens with a powerful WHOOOOSH.

The Keeper of the Magical Instrument

The WHOOSH is so powerful that it catapults Astor into another realm altogether, into outer space. He travels through space and time at a frightening speed, amid millions of twinkling stars and planets revolving in eccentric orbits past marvelous nebulae.

Breathtaking!

He is deep in awe when a beautiful woman appears in front of him, her flowing blue dress richly trimmed in gold.

"Welcome, Astor. I am Damsel Leila of the Birdsong, but you may call me Leila," she says with a luminous smile.

Astor notes the quality of her voice is that of a bird tweeting a tender melody. "A nightingale," his father would have said.

"You know my name?" asks a mystified Astor. "And where are Blanca, Cri-Cri, and Talmock?" he inquires, looking around.

"Don't worry. Your friends couldn't come along, but Blanca knew you would be in good hands. She told me your name."

"Where are we?" says Astor, unable to determine his location.

"You are in the Lyra constellation."

Although Damsel Leila's voice reminds Astor of the thrilling song of a wren claiming its territory in spring, he does not have time to think about it. He hears himself say, "Constellation? Like clusters of stars?"

"Exactly! Look everywhere," says Damsel Leila, opening her arms wide. Her sleeves float around her arms, lifted by an invisible breeze.

"Are we inside or outside?" The thought of being outside in space frightens Astor. He imagines himself falling back to Earth.

Damsel Leila of the Birdsong senses Astor's discomfort. "Have no fear. We are in the House of Cosmic Crystal. You will not fall."

A few minutes ago he was standing in the basement of The Palace of the Serene Soul, and now he is in the Lyra constellation. Astor keeps his eyes on his feet, watching stars mysteriously move by beneath him through the Cosmic Crystal.

Damsel Leila takes Astor's hand saying, "Astor, please look me in the eye."

Looking people in the eyes (except for his mother, father, and grandmother) is not easy for Astor, yet he meets Damsel Leila's gaze without effort.

Emanating from her golden-green eyes is a deep feeling of peace, and he feels it flow into his heart. Instinctively, he trusts her completely.

"Let me show you what you came for."

His curiosity is piqued because he is not sure what he is even looking for. He only knows with total certainty that he is in search of an elixir, an extraordinary elixir, to heal Lady Irena, Mistress of Singing Waters and Guardian of World Peace.

Damsel Leila takes him to a room empty except for a tall pedestal on which stands something Astor does not recognize at first.

When he gets closer, he mutters, "A lyre." Pictures his father had shown him in a book that Grandma Thea brought from Greece fill his mind.

His father also took him once to a Greek festival where a band played an array of strange instruments, and among those instruments was a lyre.

"A lyre in a glass case?" wonders Astor in a voice of surprise.

"Yes," says Damsel Leila, with a smile of satisfaction. "Not just any lyre. This is the lyre which inspired all others. In a way it is the mother of all lyres. It's called the Lyra of Cosmic Enchantment. It's in a crystal case, because crystal is the only material of sufficient purity to hold its greatness."

Astor is awestruck by the sight of the ancient instrument.

Damsel Leila starts an explanation saying, "This lyre belonged to the Greek god Hermes, who—"

Astor emerges from his state of fascination and interrupts her, saying almost mechanically, "—who created it when he was a child from the body of a large tortoise shell, by pulling strings of cow gut across it and covering it with animal hide and antelope horns."

He pauses, searching for a word. "I am not sure I know the Greek name for the tortoise. My father would."

Damsel Leila comes to the rescue. "That name is *khelus*," she says in a soft, teaching voice.

That is enough encouragement for Astor to continue. "My father taught me that Hermes traded the lyre to his half-brother, Apollo. That's how the god of music, Apollo, became master of the instrument." Astor takes a deep breath and adds, "Apollo later gave the lyre to his son, Orpheus, a great poet who also became a musician. That's all I know."

Damsel Leila of the Birdsong smiles again. "I'm very impressed by your knowledge. Your father would be proud of you."

She pauses to give the compliment time to settle.

"Let me tell you the rest of the story. Apollo gave the instrument to Orpheus when his son was just a child. Terpsichore assisted by her sisters, the Muses, taught him to play it. When Orpheus played, even Mother Nature herself would stop to listen, enraptured by his music."

Damsel Leila stops, giving a short sigh of sadness before continuing. "After Orpheus's death at the hands of the Maenads, the wild female followers of the wine god Bacchus, the Lyre was thrown into the River Hebrus, in the ancient kingdom of Byzantium. From there, it floated to the Aegean Sea and all the way to the island of Lesbos where the this lyre beached itself by the temple of Apollo."

She stops again, allowing Astor to take all that in.

"On Mount Olympus the grieving father of Orpheus convinced Zeus, god of all gods, that the Lyre should be honored by displaying it forever in the heavens. That is why Zeus placed the Lyre in its own constellation."

She stops, this time to offer a warm smile.

"You are here in the Lyre's home, between the constellations of Cygnus, the Swan and that of Hercules, whom you respect so much."

Damsel Leila extends a hand toward the instrument. "This is what you came for!"

A bewildered Astor looks at Damsel Leila saying, "I came for a cure for Lady Irena, a medicine or an elixir. What can I do with this lyre?"

"Its music is a *panacea*."

The word has an appeasing effect on Astor as he recalls his father dreaming of *a medicine that cures all illnesses.*

Yet Astor has a huge problem. "But I can't play the lyre."

"I can teach you," says Damsel Leila, who asks gently, "Don't you play the violin?"

"I do, but the lyre is very different. Until today, I've only seen a lyre once."

Damsel Leila perceives Astor's perplexity and waits for him to express his concerns.

"You can teach me to play the lyre like I play my violin?"

Damsel Leila knows that Astor is ready and a great smile illuminates her face, warming Astor's spirit. "Your father told you probably about the Muses who taught Orpheus. I also mentioned that teaching earlier," says Damsel Leila.

Astor nods.

"I am the last of the Muses and have been appointed Keeper of the Lyra. Once entrusted with that, I also inherited all the knowledge and powers of the Muses." Leila picks up the Lyre with much reverence and love. It instantly shimmers with a halo, radiating shades of green, gold, and rose.

"WOW," exclaims Astor.

Damsel Leila starts playing the Lyre.

Astor watches her with a keen eye. He notices that Leila's fingers are not plucking the strings; they simply brush against them.

They are butterflies kissing flowers.

Music engulfs the House of Cosmic Crystal, a kind of music Astor never heard before. This is different, and it stirs him in a way he never experienced until now. But he can't tell why or how.

Then, he notices that he is not hearing the music in the usual way. As a test, he plugs his ears with his fingers. The music sounds *inside* him. He feels it coursing through his veins and nerves, awakening every cell of his body.

Later, when he is more advanced in science, he will describe the music as spiraling through the helix of his DNA.

Astor is rewarded with an immediate sense of well-being. His back straightens up without any stiffening of his muscles. A light tingling in his head refines his vision and clears his thoughts.

His spirit lifts so high that he experiences a strange phenomenon: he leaves his body, soaring to a point from which he can look down on the scene. He sees Damsel Leila and himself as radiant as the halo from the Lyre.

Damsel Leila replaces the Lyre in its case with tender grace.

Instinctively, Astor knows the Lyre of Cosmic Enchantment will heal Lady Irena.

"I would like to learn to play the Lyre," Astor finally affirms. "But what can I play to cure Lady Irena? I don't know any music or song for the lyre. What kind of music heals a sick person?"

Damsel Leila senses Astor is getting frustrated again. She raises her right hand and a cool breeze blows from her palm, soothing Astor's irritation. "Be patient. All your questions will be answered."

She gestures for him to sit on a small sofa he did not notice earlier. Since it seems to be made of glass or crystal, he expects it to be hard and cold, but as he sinks into cushions covering it, he finds it pleasantly comfortable and warm.

The Lesson

"Keep your eyes on the Lyre," instructs Damsel Leila.

As soon as his eyes are focused on the Lyre, the instrument starts glowing again.

"It likes you," says Leila.

"I like it, too," responds Astor, feeling relaxed, almost sleepy.

Damsel Leila positions herself behind Astor and holds her right hand over his head.

Astor feels energy entering his head at a point right in the middle of it. Years later, he will learn that point is the *fontanel,* the soft spot in a baby's skull. He will also learn that people in India consider it a spiritual gate to the mind.

He enjoys the warm energy entering his head.

At the same moment, he sees two rays of light coming toward him from the Lyre. One of them flashes straight to a point between his eyes, just above the bridge of his nose. The other touches his chest at the top of his ribcage.

He hears music in his head, the kind he heard earlier when Leila was playing the Lyre. He has the impression that the music is being inscribed into his mind and heart. . It delivers a peculiar feeling, painless but almost ticklish.

In Astor's mind it evokes the image of an enormous number of needles delicately engraving the knowledge into his brain and heart. No, not a random number of needles—*myriad* is the word.

He wonders why.

He doesn't have to puzzle too long because the waves of incoming music give him the answer to the riddle. "Oh yes! My father told me *myriad* means ten thousand in Greek," he says with a muted chuckle that ripples in through the galaxy like the sigh of a brook gurgling into a verdant meadow, after much tumbling and cascading from a mountain.

Amusing and mystifying images—some common and many he's never seen before—keep pouring into his mind in a dizzying array of striking colors. Many of these colors are so pleasing and tasty that Astor wishes he could take a bite out of them.

"Astor, you have now all the knowledge you need to play the Lyre when you return to Earth. It's time to prepare the Lyre to go on the journey with you," says Damsel Leila.

Her words bring Astor out of his state of bliss.

"I have not touched the Lyre yet."

"No need for that! You have all that you came for."

"Do you mean I'll be able play the Lyre when I meet Lady Irena?" asks Astor.

"Oh, yes! I can tell, you will put it to good use without any more training. That is why you were chosen for this exalted labor," says Damsel Leila.

The Invisible Case

Damsel Leila gestures and a thin, glass-like flat sheet floats into the room, hovering four feet above the ground. Wondering if it is crystal, Astor discovers he can see it better if he looks at it from the corner of his eye.

"Marvelous," says Leila. "You shifted your vision. That is why you can see it. Yes, it is a crystal sheet."

Damsel Leila reverently picks up the Lyre and lays it flat on the crystal sheet, which immediately wraps itself around the instrument, sealing it into a neat case. Then it shrinks, right in front of Astor, who has a hard time believing his eyes. Lifting up the case, Leila says, "Astor, give me your hand, palm up."

When Astor does, Leila puts the case in his hand. It nestles perfectly into his palm. Astor is awed and thrilled to be holding the magically shrunken lyre in the palm of his hand.

Damsel Leila makes another gesture, and an aquamarine necklace extends from the top part of the case, allowing her to hang it around Astor's neck.

For a brief moment it rests on Astor's chest like a shining *gorget*, an armored collar similar to those that knights once wore for throat-and-chest protection.

Then it disappears.

Astor doesn't need to ask where the case went because he can feel its warmth and reassuring presence on his chest.

"Astor, you have been entrusted with the Lyra of Cosmic Enchantment and all its powers. You are ready to heal Lady Irena, Mistress of Singing Waters and Guardian of World Peace."

"But...but, how will I un...wrap the Lyra of Cosmic Enchantment?" stutters Astor.

"All you need to do is to take it with both hands, in this manner."

Damsel Leila demonstrates the move by standing behind Astor and cupping his hands under the presumed location of the now invisible Lyre.

Instantly, the Lyre glows, responding to Astor's cupped hands like a genie in a bottle answering the summons of his master.

The Lyre radiates its cosmic presence.

"Sit wherever you like. Make yourself comfortable, put the Lyre upright in your lap, and play. The Lyre and you will make an angelic team. It's that simple. Good-bye, Astor!"

Damsel Leila's eyes twinkle. Before Astor can respond, she vanishes.

The Return

Inside the castle basement, the grayish-brown metal box once again turns a serene sky blue and gives another WHOOSH.

Astor emerges from it, returning to the basement through the portal.

For a moment, Astor wonders if he can fulfill the expectation of Lord Iridio, Blanca, and the Council of Overflowing Kindness. Many thoughts, mostly doubts, invade his mind. Then, a swell of warmth on his chest reminds him of the magical presence of the Lyre of Cosmic Enchantment.

At once, all thoughts and doubts disappear.

Astor finds Blanca, Cri-Cri, and Talmock in the same positions they were when he departed. They seem frozen in time.

The time Astor spent in the Lyra constellation—meeting Damsel Leila of the Birdsong, learning to play the Lyre of Cosmic Enchantment, and bringing it back—has not passed for Astor's companions.

All that time was merely the blink of an eye for Blanca and her cohorts.

They saw Astor disappear, but before they could say or do anything, he reappeared.

The first to react are naturally the two *compadres*.

"Where have you been?" asks Cri-Cri."

"Where haven't you been?" adds Talmock.

"We were stunned by your unexpected disappearance and are startled by your sudden reappearance. We did not even have time to begin worrying. Thank heavens you are back. Are you all right?" asks Blanca.

"I have what we need for the healing. Let's do it," says Astor in an unusually firm voice.

"Yes, sir!" salutes Cri-Cri militarily.

He wants to ask what Astor has found, if anything, since Astor seems obviously empty-handed, but Blanca shakes her head firmly at Cri-Cri.

Talmock also catches the sign and its message.

Then something in the middle of Astor's chest briefly attracts Blanca's attention. She exchanges a glance of comprehension with Astor.

It is time for serious business!

Chapter Five:

The Healing

At Lady Irena's Bedside

"Through a secret corridor, I will take you to the private quarters of Lady Irena," Blanca says with a note of high hope.

Before Astor wonders about Cri-Cri and Talmock, Blanca instructs them, saying, "Please meet us there."

Astor and Blanca climb the basement steps. Shortly thereafter, Blanca indicates a passageway that takes them to a part of the palace overlooking the arroyo, and then into a set of rooms.

Lord Iridio stands by the door of the royal quarters and welcomes them. "Please come into the Sanctuary of Universal Concord."

Astor is aware that under Lord Iridio's courtesy lies his lingering sadness. He is certain however that the sadness will be healed soon.

The bedroom is enormous. It has a high glass ceiling similar to the floor of Damsel Leila's room in the Lyra constellation. *Bigger than the council chamber but smaller than the throne room*, thinks Astor.

The walls in the room shimmer a soft alabaster. Light blue drapery, the same hue as the metal safe when it is transformed in the palace basement, is hung over two tall windows. The sunlight, slanting into the room on this very early afternoon, creates a diffused aquamarine glow of delight. At the hem of the drapery where it cascades to the stone floor, the light splashes, an inviting cool pool.

In the middle of the room is a large bed with a muted rose duvet and pillows.

Astor is surprised to see the members of Council of Overflowing Kindness all gathered inside the room. He doesn't know that immediately upon his return, Blanca sent a mental message to Lord Iridio, who then summoned the entire council to Lady Irena's quarters.

Miss Tortuguita was the first to arrive, a few steps ahead of all the others. Not yet a member of the council due to her young age, she usually follows her own drummer. Today however is a different story. She reveres and adores Lady Irena, her gentle mentor, so much so that the lady's illness has pushed Miss Tortuguita into episodes of sadness.

Like a teenager, albeit a seventy-five-year-old teenager, Miss Tortuguita's excessive use of makeup is her way to mask her sadness. Sensing that a healing was surely at hand, she hurried to witness it first hand, and she came to the bedside wearing no makeup at all.

The music infuses her with a measure of good judgment that her mother tried to develop in her for years. Finally it is happening.

Entering the room and seeing Lord Iridio and the group around him, Astor tenses up at first. He has gone from spending time with one person, Damsel Leila, whose demeanor was soothing, to a group exuding a palpable anxiety.

In a reverse phenomenon, however, the anxious group relaxes when it sees Astor. They all express their fervent anticipation in a quiet hum that spreads throughout the room until Astor feels its effect.

Astor stands there until Blanca prods him by lightly touching his elbow. At that moment, he feels also the comforting warmth on his chest, a reminder of the Lyre's presence.

Then an awareness of great urgency comes over him. He senses again among the gentle councilors an unfriendly and angry spirit. The feeling is reinforced when Astor spots Newtia standing slightly apart from the others, speaking in low voice to Professor Hoot-Hooty.

Astor walks straight to Lady Irena's bedside. He imagines, more than sees, the sleeping woman. As he gets closer, he sees her head resting on a pillow but there seems to be no visible contour of her body under the duvet.

The harshness of Lady Irena's illness strains her face, clouding her legendary beauty, and bringing a pallor to her. Her dull ash blond hair is loosely spread over the pillow.

The lady's irregular breathing is a succession of sighs.

Although Astor has not met Lady Irena, he knows this is she. Having heard of her kindness and beauty, and feeling sorry for her sickly appearance, Astor makes a silent promise: *I will do all I can to heal you with the help of the Lyre of Cosmic Enchantment.*

Without waiting for an invitation, Astor sits down on a chair by the bed and makes himself comfortable, as he has been instructed to do by Damsel Leila.

To the astonishment of those present, when Astor cups his hands over his chest, a soft green light flashes. Several councilors gasp when a curious musical instrument appears on Astor's lap. A few think it might be a harp, but a rather strange harp. Somebody recognizes the instrument, and in the blink of an eye, the word *lyre* begins to be whispered.

Intrigued by such an ancient instrument, one that most of them have never seen before, much less heard, the councilors move closer to the bedside where Astor is sitting.

The Lyre now shimmers in its deep rich colors of green, gold, and rose. Hushed *ohs* and *ahs* and wide eyes express the surprise of everyone, including Lord Iridio and Blanca.

"This is the Lyre of Cosmic Enchantment," says Astor, introducing the musical instrument. His voice sounds formal, but Blanca senses it carries a note of respectful love. Moved by a mysterious force, Astor starts to play the Lyre, his fingers barely touching the strings.

Blanca marvels at Astor's dexterity.

The room fills with celestial music, awash in the Lyre's magical light. A feeling of ease engulfs all those gathered around Lady Irena's bed.

Then a curious thing happens. Under the music's spell some of those present begin to react with unexpected longing.

Señora Tortuga suddenly desires a particular lettuce, not iceberg, heavens forbid, but Belgian endive. She tastes in her mouth that crispy lettuce, to which a young woman with a European accent introduced her fifty years ago.

Miss Mariposa envisions a rare flower from her beloved Costa Rica. Located deep inside the flower's long-necked corolla, the pure ecstasy of its sugar requires the expert unfolding of her proboscis. For the first time, her proboscis starts pulsing to the lively beat of a guitar.

Talmock itches to perform a song he heard on a long-ago night under a full-moon. He heard it from a lovely female nightingale, a traveling avian minstrel. She had been blown off course by a storm, and exhausted, landed on the highest branch of Talmock's regal dwelling, a tall oak tree. Talmock welcomed the nightingale and provided her with a meal of fruit and seeds, concluding with a rich dessert—a piece of pie he had pilfered from a neighbor's windowsill.

After a brief rest, Milady—as Talmock nicknamed her because he could not pronounce her foreign name—thanked her host with the most enchanting repertoire he ever heard. Their encounter was barely longer than her song, for the next afternoon Milady was dead. While Talmock was away on mockingbird business, a hawk grabbed the nightingale as she was flying to a nearby pond for a sip of water.

A heartbroken Talmock often recalls the memory of his Milady, whose songs he wanted to learn. He is barely able to control his urge to start singing the only song of hers he knows.

Cri-Cri's missing leg tingles as if it were still there. Having experienced that sensation before, he knows it to be unreal. Now he looks down and can't believe his eyes: his leg *is* there, as powerful and real as before. He wants to throw away his cane but controls himself as well.

Mantra joins her forelegs into that praying gesture from which she derives her name. Reminiscing over the several dozen husbands she has eaten over the years, she offers them a silent prayer of thanks and calls on high blessings for them. She promises not to eat any husband from now on; just to throw out the bad ones. Her green livery glows healthy and beautiful.

Toady-dy, master of trance, sits massive and calm. The music creates an electric tension on his skin, which long ago had gone dry. Thanks to an untapped abundance of a natural ointment that would have delighted any sun-loving human, Toady-dy's skin regenerates, moist and elastic.

Professor Hoot-Hooty, a permanent and respected member of the council, rarely attends its meetings. Today, he is present, his big eyes narrowed, almost closed, as he probes inside himself for some mysterious knowledge. Soon his eyes reopen to their normal large size, infused with a glint of satisfaction.

Suddenly, his huge, square glasses, which usually move from side to side in a measured fashion, uncontrollably increase their speed, blurring Professor Hoot-Hooty's vision. He has no other option than to physically stop them with both wings. That is a method he often uses when his twin owlets run amok.

Next to him, Newtia presents his usual impenetrable self, quiet and immobile, eyes closed. The music does not appear to affect him, unless it affects him so much that it has put him into a reverie. Difficult to read, he is a true enigma.

Blanca sits serene, confident that the healing will take place. Yet she can't help exhibiting a touch of apprehension by blinking her eyes in rapid sets of three and drumming her right front paw on her chest.

Lord Iridio sits alone on a chair on the other side of the bed, close to Lady Irena's head. "So that I can hear her breathe," he confided once to Blanca. Bent forward to closely mind each breath of Lady Irena, he truly does look benevolent.

When Blanca had introduced Astor to him in the Throne Room, Lord Iridio had displayed his inner emotional turmoil in the dimness of his rainbow and in the erratic flashing of the light coming from his forehead, throat, and chest.

Now, everything changes before Astor's eyes.

Meanwhile at the Aquatic Center

At that moment, at a table in the park outside the Aquatic Center, Astor's mother is still reading her medical journal.

All of a sudden, a mysterious new tune arises in her mind.

The music evolves into a serenade that enchants her, filling her heart with serenity.

That's how I want to feel, every day! She tells herself.

∾

At Lady Irena's bedside, Astor is transported by the beautiful music he is playing. At one point, though, he doubts he is even playing. So he stops for a second and immediately the music slows almost to a halt, turning into a wail.

Everyone in the room feels the change, perceiving it as a special part of the Concert of Healing.

Promptly returning his fingers to the Lyre's strings, Astor no longer has any doubt. *He* is playing the most spell-binding music ever heard on Earth.

Astor is in the habit of closing and opening his eyes while playing his violin; and he falls into that habit during this concert. He closes his eyes for a few seconds, and when he reopens them, Astor notices from the corner of his eye a slight movement in the bed. He does not pay it much attention until it happens once more.

A few bars more, he notices the form of Lady Irena under the covers.

That form was not visible when he first sat down; he is sure of that.

Has the emaciated body of Lady Irena miraculously regained the flesh and muscles it lost during her illness? Astor muses. He decides to keep an eye on Lady Irena. As he continues playing, the strained features of Lady Irena's face slowly start relaxing and rejuvenating; her whole face changes, shifting from deathly pallor to a healthy shade of pink.

In a sudden move, Lady Irena sits up in the bed, something she has not done in months. Then, just as suddenly, she starts coughing, the sort of cough that alarms mothers.

That immediately alerts Miss Rosette, the palace nurse. The pink mouse with the white apron and a powder-blue bonnet, was standing by, until then hidden by the flowing drapes. As Lady Irena's cough turns into retching, Miss Rosette materializes on the other side of the bed with a bucket in her paws.

Skillfully, she catches Lady Irena's vomit the second it starts. It's a disgusting mixture of dark-brown goo and grayish-white foam that comes out in three violent bursts.

The bursts freeze everyone in a horrible fright for Lady Irena's health—everyone, that is, except for Astor, Blanca, and Professor Hoot-Hooty, who understand the healing process is taking place.

Astor notices a more radical change happening in Lady Irena. As though flowing from the palette of a mysterious painter, an array of colors blossoms over her face. Radiating a golden glow, her hair turns honey-blond.

Is that its original color? Astor asks himself.

Then Lady Irena passes her hands over her face. *A gesture of cleansing,* rejoices Blanca. Losing the harshness caused by Lady Irena's grave illness, her features regain their exquisite lines, as if chiseled by an invisible sculptor.

Lady Irena looks around and sees the faces of her closest friends in the House of Iridio. These faces are usually relaxed or moving from one emotion to another without dwelling on anything negative.

This time the faces are tense.

Lady Irena realizes her illness is the cause of her friends' distress. Her only desire now is to erase the tension she sees in their expressions and pass on her gathering sense of well-being to the noble souls assembled here.

She smiles. As her smile spreads into a sunbeam of a grin all over her face, it is at once reflected on the faces of all those around her.

So subtle is the pattern that they are unaware of it until some feel an sense of elation. They look at each other relieved, truly relieved, and nod their appreciation. Their nods evoke for Astor the rippling of grass under the gentle breath of an afternoon breeze.

At this moment Lord Iridio magically regains the full splendor of his rainbow colors with their eternal powers:

Red suggesting passion for life and heat for cold winters.

Orange offering warmth and temperance in all actions.

Yellow sending sunny rays for harvests and hopes.

Green dispensing soothing and healing to body and soul.

Blue promoting peace through dialog.

Indigo inviting all to conviviality, and

Violet advocating harmony and spirituality.

All these colors glow around him, magnificent and healthy.

The lights emanating from Lord Iridio's forehead, throat, and chest are equally dazzling.

Lord Iridio, having regained his royal composure, picks up Lady Irena's hands, and kisses them. Then, still holding them in his own, he joyously addresses the gathered group. "Confirming the old Prophecy of Fire, a miracle has taken place before our own eyes. We are most grateful to Astor for his healing prowess. Now Lady Irena needs to recover completely from her ordeal. Let us therefore disperse and gather tomorrow morning for a celebration in the Hall of Eclectic Leisure and Minute Pleasures."

With happiness in their hearts, the councilors bid Lady Irena good-bye and leave the room, exchanging hushed compliments, words of satisfaction, and best wishes. After nearly everyone departs, the Lyre promptly returns to its hiding place on Astor's chest.

Lord Iridio shakes Astor's hand with great warmth, "I am so grateful to you, Astor, more than I can express right now. I'll see you tomorrow," he says with tears of happiness in his eyes. "Blanca, please take care of our Honored Guest."

∾

Blanca quickly returns Astor to his mother, who does not show any concern for his absence.

"I don't know…can I…come back tomorrow?" Astor asks Blanca.

"Yes, I know Sunday is a day of rest for your mom; she prefers to do nothing. But have faith," she says smiling.

"OK," says Astor, by now accustomed to the unexpected in these last few days.

Astor eats his lunch with much gusto, delighting his mother.

Shortly afterwards they are on their way home.

∾

In bed Astor pulls out his laptop, a gift from his grandmother, and does some research about depression on the Internet.

He finds that the condition is often caused, among other factors, by a chemical imbalance in the brain. Correcting that imbalance appears to him a formidable undertaking. Besides medicine, he wonders, what may do that?

Could music, for example? Could it change the structure of the chemicals released in the brain or substitute other chemicals?

His active imagination triggers a multitude of images that pop into his mind.

Recalling a drawing that his father simplified for him, he recognizes brain cells called neurons, with long and bizarre extensions called dendrites, being born in abundance while old pathways are clipped away. For a while his head is full of short-lived images speeding by on his mind screen like galaxies in space.

Astor wonders where these images emanate from—the Lyre? He gets no confirmation. Then the show is over and he goes to sleep, his laptop beside him.

The Day After

Sunday morning, when Astor comes out of his room, he encounters the greatest surprise of his life.

In the past, on her day off, his mother sleeps in the morning until ten and spends another two hours in bed, alternating between dozing off and waking up. Then around noon she drags herself downstairs for lunch. In fact, lunch is anything remotely edible left in the fridge from meals Grandmother Thea prepared during her visits.

Astor expects to tiptoe around the kitchen. That is how he avoids waking his mother before she has had enough sleep, while fixing himself some cereal with apricot juice for breakfast.

That's what he intended to do.

Instead, the aroma of pancakes with blueberries delights his sense of smell.

When he sits down at the table, his mother appears with a large bag of raisins from Corinth, a gift his grandmother brings back from Greece every year, to sprinkle on top of the pancakes. His mother, already dressed, says to him, "I thought we might want to spend more time at the arroyo. You seem to enjoy going there. For sure it has a pleasant effect on me. I don't understand it, but I love it. It's the mystery of the arroyo."

Yeah, it is the Arroyo of Mystery all right, thinks Astor joyfully to himself.

The Hall of Eclectic Leisure and Minute Pleasures

At nine-thirty Sunday morning, Astor and his mother are back at the arroyo, where Blanca is waiting. Again Blanca puts Astor's mother in an alpha state—a trance from which she won't awaken until she and Astor return.

Crossing the street and entering the path west of the Aquatic Center, Blanca and Astor walk with purpose. Within ten minutes they arrive at the Hall of Eclectic Leisure and Minute Pleasures inside the palace.

The Hall is in a huge cavern, bigger than anything Astor has ever seen before. *Maybe three hundred feet long and hundred and fifty wide,* he mentally calculates. Two aisles divide the Hall into three areas with the central part about twice the width of the two side sections.

The Hall's soaring ceiling is painted with such a real-looking blue sky and white wispy clouds that Astor expects the three enormous chandeliers hanging from those clouds to drift away with them.

The four walls are covered with murals, pastoral scenes of rabbits grazing on the gentle hillocks or flocks of birds on their way to roost at sunset - scenes of the four seasons:

In Spring a multitude of birds are busy. Here, perched on a branch, an elegant male towhee is wooing a dull brown female, invisible in the underbrush until she flutters her wings in approval. Over there, pairs of birds are discussing a nest site, while others already in full-construction phase carry twigs. At the tip of a flimsy branch, a female hummingbird is enhancing the softness of her home with a delicate moss, her thimble-size nest safely hanging from a spider thread.

In Summer, when the sun is unwilling to set and the Arroyo Seco comes into its true meaning of "dry creek," most animals rest in the shade, panting. In the background, an emaciated young coyote is venturing into a human neighborhood, famished, in search of water and whatever else comes its way.

In Fall, squirrels stash away acorns in so many locations that, comes spring, their forgetfulness will lead to an abundance of newly sprouting oaks. In long military columns, ants carry to ensile leaves, grains, and other edibles.

In Winter, even without much rain and no snow for sure, a sense of pseudo-hibernation, mostly a slow-down, descends upon most of the rodent clans. Above, in the treetops, parrots are raucously complaining about the lack of food and asking for directions to any new find. The animals are so well rendered that for a brief moment, Astor believes these are real animals coming through the walls.

The infinite assortment of hues and tones that turn the walls into gigantic murals continuously shift and change. As Astor lingers to look at them for a moment, their colors and shadows slowly turn into new scenes.

They are paintings with capricious minds, he thinks, amused.

∾

The Hall is full. Astor never imagined so many animals in one location, certainly not at the zoo. He thinks of Noah's Ark, and even then, *Wasn't there only one pair of each species?* he wonders to himself.

The Council of Overflowing Kindness is seated in the front row of the Hall, facing a raised, sky-blue podium. The podium supports two imposing golden thrones upholstered in a serene green. Astor is happy to see the twins, Hooty-Tooty and Tooty-Hooty. They are quietly sitting between their father, Professor Hoot-Hooty, and an owl in an elegant light-blue dress, a flowery corsage, and large pink glasses. She seems in a state of meditation, while conveying a subtle air of distinction.

"Who's that owl with Professor Hoot-Hooty and the twins?" asks Astor.

"Oh! That's Dame Hoota-Tooha, the twins' mother," says Blanca. "She is a devoted wife who stays at home to take care of the household, the twins, and her husband, the professor, whom she lovingly calls her oldest child."

She smiles before going on. "She has earned several advanced degrees; one in molecular biology, which she easily translates into healthy cooking, and another in quantum physics. This one, she says she enjoys applying to metaphysics, philosophy, and the arts. Needless to say, Professor Hoot-Hooty does not concoct anything without her lively and informed input. He is brilliant, and she is his equal. That's why she has been appointed Confidante Extraordinaire to Lady Irena and Advisor Emeritus to Lord Iridio.

"Every year Lady Irena and she organize the Annual Convention of Femaleness at which all females in the kingdom, regardless of their age or species, gather to reaffirm their critical importance to life. Of course, there are always long talks about their concerns."

"You must be…" interrupts Astor.

"Yes, I am one of the organizers, but I'm sorry, this is not the time for that conversation," says Blanca humbly.

She cuts Astor off because the subject is dear to her, and she needs more time to explain it to him properly.

The twins, elegant in and proud of their light-gray suits, baseball caps, and triangular glasses with magenta-tinted lenses, discreetly wave to Astor and Blanca, who wave back in the same manner.

Seated behind the council are the official delegations of distinguished guests, each in the company of an ambassador with jewels and marks of honor on head or chest.

From various parts of the world, there are antelopes, buffalos, cheetahs, deer, crocodiles, elephants, elks, emus, giraffes, laughing and spotted hyenas, jaguars, kangaroos, lions, ocelots, green mamba snakes and black mambas, so named for their black mouths, pythons, zebras, a mountain lion——a lonely resident of the San Gabriel Mountains—and others that Astor doesn't know.

The guests have arrived as mysteriously as they were invited, Astor supposes. He doesn't think it's the right time to ask Blanca about it. *Maybe another day*, he thinks.

They are seated in alphabetical order, in accordance with palace protocol. Their conversations are subdued and dignified, their movements deliberate, slow and elegant.

What amazes Astor is that they all sit side by side, talking like old friends who haven't seen each other for a long time, even though they might be old enemies - predators and prey.

On both sides of the aisles, against the walls, as far as the eye can see, in no specific order except species, are tittering groups of raccoons, dogs, opossums, rabbits, frogs, toads, and creatures Astor cannot not identify.

There is a general feeling of intense expectation, yet the audience is abuzz with good-humor and self restraint. Hushed conversations are punctuated by nodding heads, clicking tongues, fluttering wings, and blinking eyes.

The avian ilk perches in rafters located below the ceiling and across the width of the hall. On seven high bars, dozens of green parrots with yellow-and-red heads, as well as one lonely white cockatoo, are perched in complete silence.

That pleasantly surprises Astor, who loves the parrots' beautiful plumage but can't stand their "croaking," as he calls their squawking, especially when trees near his house teem with their raucous presence in the mornings.

Immediately below them, twelve scrub jays, in their elegant blue suits and gray vests, are perched, silently eyeing the whole scene with a satisfied sense of ownership. It's another surprise for Astor who knows that the usual reaction of the jays would be to attack any territorial intruder.

A subdued twittering leads Astor's eyes to a row of splendid ruby-crowned kinglets, just below the jays. For the celebration they proudly display their magnificent crowns that are often hidden except in times of mating.

Then Astor's attention is caught by a perch populated by an unusual duo of avian species: a teapot of two dozen California towhees all clad in dull brown overalls evokes a gathering of a religious order punctuating its prayer with faint "tss, tss," melodiously tweeted. Next to them, a small bevy of silent black-hooded phoebes projects an eerie image of a conspiracy being hatched before his eyes.

The two species are separated by a single black-hooded bird, obviously of the phoebe family. Astor, however, is not fooled.

He learned from his father that the white-streaked black back and wings, along with the white chest and underbelly flanked by a generous dusting of cinnamon, identify this pretty bird as a male towhee.

"They are all residents of the arroyo," says Astor to himself

Birds of all kinds are flying in the space, underneath the rafters but above the aisles and in the rows behind the Council. Hummingbirds are showing off, performing daring acrobatics and elegant aerial ballets that involve hovering, high-speed-diving, and backward flying.

Butterflies in stunning colors, green flies, red, blue, and transparent dragonflies, and fireflies buzz above a special zone set aside for insects.

For evident reasons, it's a zone forbidden to the birds.

As soon as Blanca and Astor arrive, Master Circonius, the newly appointed Deputy Chief of Protocol, appears. He is a rather tall bird with a purplish-green sheen to his black plumage. His red bill and legs identify him as a black stork. A peppy young man who has just come into adulthood, he carries a thin staff inlaid with mother-of-pearl and wears a silver necklace adorned with cowries—the mark of his high position.

"Would Miss Blanca and our Honored Guest, Astor, follow me to their seats?" he says with a nod of greeting. He takes them to the front row where two seats are reserved for them among the Council of Overflowing Kindness.

On the way, Master Circonius proudly informs Astor and Blanca that he has spent the past several hours seating the foreign delegations according to protocol. He went on to say that an official surfeit of skunks arrived in their distinctive white and black suits and tails surrounded by only an incredibly light smell. "Would you believe that I found myself wanting more of that smell?" he adds sternly.

"*Is he joking?*, muses Astor.

"I hope so!" answers Blanca.

Hardly have Blanca and Astor been seated when the tantara of trumpets sounds, intent and imperious. A gaze of six raccoon announces the approach of the royal couple by blowing into silver trumpets twice their heights. In gray suits with black lapels and their permanent black masks, they look more like partygoers than court officials.

An unusually tall bird, Sir Ibis of the Nile, ambles ten feet ahead of the royal couple. A striking gold necklace, set with a large diamond surrounded by rubies and emeralds, hangs heavily around his neck. In his left wing, he holds a thick staff of dark ebony topped by a carved-ivory unicorn head.

These two objects are the insignia of his high status as Chief of Protocol and Perceptive Advisor to Lord Iridio.

His gait is slow and official, and one can see that he is also slow due to his venerable age. The immaculate white plumage of his youth now displays long streaks of gray. In spite of a defective left eye, Sir Ibis stubbornly refuses to wear glasses. Instead, he dons, at his own pleasure, a strange monocle perched high on his beak.

At first, he had some concerns about his monocle because in order to keep the contraption in place, he has to hold his beak higher than normal. That gives him an air of unintended arrogance. While everyone in the arroyo is aware of his kindness, many poke fun at him by imitating his haughty appearance. He became proud of the device though, when Professor Hoot-Hooty remarked that it made *him* look professorial.

Sir Ibis slowly climbs onto the podium followed by the royal couple, whom he respectfully directs to their seats with an expansive gesture of his right wing.

Then, in a distinguished and slightly high-pitched voice—a sure sign of hearing loss for those who can read it—he announces, "Their Highnesses, Lord Iridio, Master of the Rainbow and Protector of the Arroyo, and Lady Irena, Mistress of Singing Waters and Guardian of World Peace."

He then moves to the side of the podium.

The crowd jumps to its feet, claws, and paws and starts clapping while chanting a hypnotic, "*Ner Iridio wa Nebt Irena Maranathain!*"

"What are they saying?" asks Astor.

"In a mixture of ancient languages, they are chanting 'Lord Iridio and Lady Irena have come," says Blanca.

The hall is filled with the sounds of a celebration the likes of which have never been seen before, and who knows how many joyous events have taken place there?

The celebration continues, loud and cheerful, as the royal pair proceeds to their respective thrones on the podium. Lady Irena takes her seat, but Lord Iridio remains standing.

The noise only stops when Lord Iridio raises a hand. "I have the infinite pleasure to inform you that Lady Irena is no longer ill. She has regained her health, as you can see for yourselves."

Lady Irena rises from her seat and steps forward, graciously bowing to her subjects. In her delightful voice, which matches her beauty she says, "Beloved friends, I am here alive and well in front of you, thanks to the heroism of a young boy seated here among us."

"A young boy?" exclaim many attendees who have experienced unpleasant run-ins with young members of the human species.

"Yes, a *heroic* boy!" continues Lady Irena. "Passing through an ancient cosmic portal, which is located inside the palace but has been unknown to us until now, he traveled to a distant galaxy to bring back what healed me. I will let him show you what that is. I'll just gratefully add that I owe this boy my life."

She steps back but remains standing, too.

Two fast-running brown squirrels with green baseball caps, orange overalls, and bushy purple tails immediately deliver two seats, placing them to one side of Lady Irena's throne.

Blanca mentally advises Astor that they are to move to these two new seats as soon as Sir Ibis bows in their direction; which he does immediately.

Without haste nor delay Astor and Blanca climb onto the podium, bow and curtsy to the royal couple and stand next to Lady Irena' throne.

Lord Iridio introduces them with great warmth.

"Here is our Honored Guest and beloved friend, Astor, and here is our dearest Miss Blanca, who discovered him in the arroyo. There are more from our own kingdom involved in this amazing tale; they will be recognized later."

The hall erupts again into applause and joyful sounds of all sorts. Lord Iridio sits down, as do Lady Irena, Miss Blanca, and Astor.

Sir Ibis, who has remained standing to one side, firmly supported by his ebony staff, steps forward and lifts his beak to adjust his monocle. That stops the applause and initiates a wave of beak- and snout-lifting imitations.

Pleased, Sir Ibis's good eye blinks three times in acknowledgment of the audience's good-natured behavior. His monocle adjusted, Sir Ibis announces in his raspy, high-pitched voice, "The festivities start with the debut performance of the Avian Choir of the Arroyo, a newly formed group. It is directed by none other than the Honorable Councilor Talkie-Mockie, our Talmock. He was one of the adventurers who discovered the magic to cure Lady Irena, as mentioned by Lord Iridio. We salute him for that! Here is for this auspicious occasion a… World Premiere!"

Upon hearing "world premiere," which is their cue, twenty slender mockingbirds file in, very professional in their pale-gray, almost-white suits, each enhanced by a pink carnation. They walk in straight lines like arrows, an oddity for mockingbirds who are a facetious, undisciplined species always ready to mimic a voice or a sound.

The appearance of the mockingbirds triggers a set of good memories.

Astor warmly remembers the succession of mockingbirds that for the last five years have taken over his own small backyard. Their musical repertoire ranges from imitating a cat's meow to re-engineering Ravel's, a piece his father played religiously every Sunday afternoon.

Astor smiles, recalling how puzzled his dad had been one warm summer afternoon when he heard the mockingbird's rendition.

Papa Archimedes, as Astor sometimes called his father, expressed his irritation in a vigorous shout. "Who is acting up now?" he bellowed, convinced that a neighbor was mocking his beloved music. After some investigating, he broke into roaring laughter and applause when he realized the music came from the top of their cypress tree, the favored perch of the mockingbird.

"That's my bird," he said approvingly.

Once the choir is seated -ten of them perch on the first riser and ten arrange themselves in front of them on the stage floor—the Honorable Councilor Talkie-Mockie enters, resplendent in a lilac-colored suit with black tie and a black cummerbund divided in the middle by a bold pink stripe.

He strides to the podium, which is thirty feet from the choir. Talmock raises a wing, and the choir immediately launches into an amazing performance of sounds, pitches, and calls.

The audience expects the seemingly random collection of sounds to degenerate into musical chaos. Yet a sophisticated harmony prevails, confirming the high quality of a well-rehearsed group.

The next number starts with the ten mockingbirds on the riser humming softly, accompanying the ten on the floor who launch into a long dance. The mockingbirds love to display their wings, rounding them to show volume and fluttering them to indicate depth, height, and spiritual dimensions. The number concludes with the notes of a lively medley. The crowd jumps up and down with delight, and some spontaneously dance in the aisles.

The last applause is still dying away when a group of ten portly crows, elegant in their black tuxedos and white bow ties, marches in. Sporting shiny white beaks, the well-fed birds look enormous, even unfriendly.

The ten mockingbirds that just finished their dance hasten to their seats on the riser above their brothers.

In marked contrast to the streamlined mockingbirds, the crows now loom over them, a gang of humongous toughs.

That intrigues an apprehensive audience.

In the first number the crows show their mastery of the low notes in ten short solos superbly performed between their opening and ending songs. Marveling at the skill of each crow, the audience rewards them with much applause at the end of each number.

Then Talmock raises his wings, making a cryptic circle over his head. Many in the audience wonder about the gesture, but it is apparently clear to the Avian Choir.

The ten mockingbirds on top the riser descend to one side of the stage where, joined by their ground colleagues, they start singing a melody.

The crows move to the opposite side and pick up the same tune but in a deeper register.

After a few minutes of point and counterpoint, the mockingbirds resume their previous dance routine in the center of the stage. This time they dance without a pattern.

They are truly twenty birds out of control!!!

The crows look at each other in disbelief, betraying their surprise with cawing that sounds like questions. Even Talmock looks pained, holding his head and shielding his eyes from the sight.

The magic kicks in when Talmock dejectedly raises his wings, this time to express his loss of the choir's direction.

Still singing their questions, the crows form a circle to one side, powwowing briefly then going into action.

All this time the mockingbirds are having great fun, mimicking other birds and animals, even aping human dances.

The crows move in, encircling the mockingbirds while singing the same song in their deeper voices. At times, one of the crows tries to imitate a mockingbird's high-pitched note. The result, a musical fiasco, triggers laughter from the audience.

Then, the crows open their wings, rounding them over the mockingbirds and herding the small birds into a circle at the center of the stage.

For a brief moment, the mockingbirds disappear under the crows' wings, their voices drowned by the formidable cawing of the crows.

Tension overwhelms the audience as it wonders about the fate of the mockingbirds. The audience goes quiet. Small birds, who are always on the lookout for predators, have tears in their eyes.

Suddenly, a flutter of wings and the rumble of a song sound so swiftly that many in the audience cannot recall it happening. The result is incredible—each of the ten crows bears two mockingbirds, one on each wing. None of the twenty mockingbirds is unaccounted for.

They are all there!

Perched high on the shoulders of the crows, the mockingbirds start a victory song celebrating a triumph over a heftier and mightier enemy.

Good sports, the crows applaud, and while the mockingbirds still sing, the crows quietly move into a fast circling and snaking dance to conclude the show.

The final bow takes place with the mockingbirds still perched on the crows' shoulders.

The audience jumps to its feet, roaring and clapping with delight, relieved of the fearful tension that gripped it for a while. It takes a some time before the audience's cheering, whistling, clapping, and dancing finally stop.

Meanwhile, the members of the Avian Choir of the Arroyo stand there saying a modest, "Thank you."

Finally Talmock bows and exits in a dignified manner. Then the choir files out, mockingbirds first, followed by the crows.

∽

Sir Ibis of the Nile moves forward to announce, "It is time to call on another member of the council who was also part of Lady Irena's healing. I now give you the Honorable Crickety-Crick, our Cri-Cri, descendant of the legendary Earl Tamani, Protector of the Cricket Hall of Fame."

Cri-Cri enters the stage wearing burnt sienna-colored tights, a pale green shirt with a darker green tie, and a light orange waistcoat. As usual, his beloved tam-o'-shanter is tilted toward his left eye. An electric-blue cane in his right hand completes the image of an elegant, cool dude.

For a warm-up, Cri-Cri starts with one of his least-known tap-dancing routines. He's taken only three steps when he falls. His cane goes one way and the tam-o'-shanter another, fortunately both within reach.

He quickly stands up but falls again after another three steps. The audience loves it, thinking that he is performing a parody of his own dance.

Cri-Cri, however, concludes that he does not yet have full control of his new leg. For a very brief moment, he even wonders if his new limb hasn't come with its own mind.

Bah! he thinks to himself. *A leg with its own mind—that's all I need.*

As a talented performer, always aware of his audience, he decides to give the people what they want, namely laughter. So he continues the dance, this time embracing a spoof of his own spirited dance.

Every time they are thrown into the air together, the cane and the tam-o'-shanter fall awkwardly to the ground. Obviously, that's the behavior of a drunk, or at least of an inexperienced dancer, when actually it's a clever artistic ploy.

After a few minutes of the spoof, Cri-Cri is confident that he finally has gained full mastery over his new limb. He decides to conclude with his most famous number. This time, before the cane and the tam-o'-shanter fall on the stage, each one performs a series of fancy air acrobatics separately into different directions.

Suddenly, they discover each other, two rivals vying for the attention and applause of the audience. Instantly, they are dueling across the stage. Then, exhausted, they fall to the floor in a warm embrace.

When Cri-Cri bows, the crowd explodes into a roar of appreciation. It takes a while for the cheering, whistling, and clapping to stop.

Sir Ibis of the Nile, supported by his ebony staff, steps forward and waits until all the hullabaloo dies down. He lifts his beak and adjusts his eyeglass.

The spectators, pleasantly satiated by the entertainment, are expecting some important announcement.

They are not disappointed.

Sounding solemn, Sir Ibis announces, "Now here is our Honorable Blanca, Confidante of Lady Irena. She was a key player in this saga."

With his right wingtip, he indicates Blanca, who moves forward and curtsies to the audience.

"Blanca! Blanca! Blanca!" chant the audience members, who know her well and are fond of her.

She stands smiling and waits for the applause and cheers to stop. "I have the great pleasure to introduce to you Astor, the real hero of this incredible saga. He is going to give us a taste of the medicine that healed Lady Irena."

She returns to her seat.

Perplexed, an African jackal asks his coyote neighbor, "What kind of medicine would that be?"

"And I wonder what form its administration is going to take?" responds the local neighbor. "Would it be released in the air like a perfume or a gas?" They just laughed, waiting to see.

Astor's Performance

"As-tor! As-tor! As-tor!" clamors the audience.

Astor comes forward, and one of the squirrels, standing immobile on the side of the podium, carries Astor's seat to the center of the stage.

Astor bows to the audience. Like an experienced musician, he sits down with his hands clasped on his lap and glances at the audience.

He slowly raises his clasped hands and, with an even movement, opens his arms. There is a green flash and—

"OHHH!"

Astonishment from the crowd ripples across the Hall of Eclectic Leisure and Minute Pleasures. A multitude of eyes, beaks, and mouths open widely, some wildly.

Astor holds himself erect and breathes deeply. As soon as he closes his eyes, his fingers tingle, excited and ready to brush against the Lyre's strings. He starts playing, his fingers skimming over the strings like a late summer breeze over a lake's waters.

All eyes and beaks and mouths still open, finally close, and the audience relaxes. Although the attendees came in great spirits, there are some who carry anger, sadness, or resentment in their hearts. These feelings are part of their daily lives, and those who bear them are unaware that, even at this moment of celebration, the feelings weigh heavily upon them.

The music sounds heavenly, its melodious kindness received by everyone according to their state of mind.

Many hear it instantly, while others remain deaf to it, entangled in their own problems; but it does not take long before they hear it too.

Those sad or pessimistic feel a warming sense of joy that lifts them into happiness; at this point they are ready to dance with anyone around them. This is especially true for the large contingent of teen-agers: cottontails, squirrels, raccoons, and opossums, who often feel misunderstood in a senseless world.

Those with anger and resentment receive a cooling flow of energy that washes away their stewing violence and gives them peace of mind; they are willing to talk with and ask forgiveness from those who angered them and felt the weight of that anger.

This is notably the case with an old beaver, the last of an ancient line that lived in the arroyo long before the construction of the concrete dam upstream.

The beaver is so angry at life that no one passes his den without being pelted with whatever is at hand, including his feces. He is particularly unfriendly toward a family of raccoons that lives in a nearby tree. Now, awash in the healing music, he starts crying, ashamed for the stinking garbage and the unspoken misery he has dumped for so long on his neighbors.

Astor plays the first piece for a short time. Then, gently directed by the Lyre, he begins to play a more lively tune. Although he is sure he never has heard the tune before, Astor feels some connection to it.

Glancing out at the immense Hall, Astor notices, to his great surprise, every member of the audience humming or singing along. Without looking behind him, he is convinced that Lord Iridio, Lady Irena, Blanca, and all those assembled on the podium are also singing the melody.

Later, Professor Hoot-Hooty will explain to Astor the compelling reason for that gigantic sing-along. The melody is a musical rendering of the sounds heard by every fetus in the womb or the egg.

It is a primal tune, common to all species.

As Astor looks out from the stage, a faint haze of green, golden, and rose hues floats through the hall. Children in the audience are secretly convinced genies are enjoying themselves, creating the colors and mutating them at will.

Every time Astor plays a note, a different color blooms. With each note reflecting a color, a tune transforms them into a short-lived painting. Euphonious notes, pleasant-sounding ones, engender a dazzling palette of colors. A reoccurring color is green, and Astor identifies it as the color of healing because it not only soothes the audience; it transports the listeners into a state of never-before-encountered bliss.

Awash in the colors swirling around Astor, the audience sees in him the image of a young Lord Iridio.

Shortly afterward, the flow of music starts to slow, indicating to Astor that the performance is ending.

Finally, the Lyre falls silent.

A Cosmic Event

The contented audience has barely realized the music is over when a magical event occurs. A smaller lyre suddenly emerges from the Lyre of Cosmic Enchantment.

"OHHH!" gasps the audience again.

At the moment, no one quite understands what's happening.

∾

Years later participants, relating the event to their children and grandchildren, would say they attended the *cosmic event when the Lyre gave birth to a baby lyre*. As one may expect, these stories would be laughed at, and the storytellers themselves very rarely believed. Teenage children would disregard their parents' stories and the chronicles they tell of that time, discounting them as the fantasies of old fogies.

The only captive audience parents and grandparents would find are the very young children who would sit spellbound at their knees, wishing and dreaming of being there at that miraculous moment.

∾

Instinctively, Astor knows the new lyre is a personal gift from Damsel Leila of the Birdsong and the Lyre of Cosmic Enchantment.

"*Thank you*," he whispers, willing his message to reach Damsel Leila's mind. "*I am delighted and deeply honored*," he adds with a profound reverence.

The Lyre of Cosmic Enchantment strums a melodious sound and disappears in a flash of fuchsia light. The baby lyre spontaneously nestles against Astor's chest, hanging invisibly from his neck as its mother had done.

∾

Fully aware of the audience's state of awe, Sir Ibis seizes the opportunity. Clearing his voice twice, he announces, "Please stand as Lord Iridio, Lady Irena, our hero, Astor, Miss Blanca, and the Honorable Council of Overflowing Kindness leave the auditorium."

All stand to salute the departure of the royal couple, Astor, Blanca, and the council. In so doing, the audience also expresses its loving gratitude to be living under the rule of such wise leaders.

Lord Iridio is mindful of an ancient adage that *a full stomach makes the head sing with satisfaction*. As a conclusion to the festivities, the ruler has decided to turn this proverb on its head: since the attendees' heads are already full of song and music, it is time to fill their stomachs as well.

As they exit in deep calm and total discipline, each attendee is given a basket of food and invited to join a picnic set up just outside the castle in the arroyo. Every basket is consistent with the receiver's diet. Mistakes are not acceptable and certainly not allowed. No worms for turtles, and no lettuce or endive—even Belgian—for robins.

Chapter Six:

All Is Well...At Last

The Confession

In his slow and formal trailblazing style, Sir Ibis guides Lord Iridio, Lady Irena, Astor, Blanca, and the members of the Council of Overflowing Kindness along the grand hallway into the Hall of the Rainbow Throne.

The assembled councilors and friends have just taken their positions around Lord Iridio's and Lady Irena's thrones when an incredibly disturbing event occurs.

Suddenly, a member of the council falls to the ground and starts rolling from side to side, apparently the victim of a seizure.

His limbs twitch in spastic movements.

His claws keep grabbing and releasing invisible objects.

His dilated pupils and staring eyes make him look so terrifying that he even scares some of his council colleagues.

It's Newtia.

Professor Hoot-Hooty looks upon his colleague and friend with dismay. Quickly recovering from the shock, he makes a move toward his rescue.

A gesture from Lord Iridio stops him.

Lord Iridio then opens his hands to summon an elegant hyacinth macaw carrying a beautifully gilded armchair with serene green upholstery.

Astor understands that he is being invited by Lord Iridio to play the lyre once more. This unexpected request takes Astor by surprise; it even makes his nose twitch, leading Astor to wonder if he is becoming a rabbit. *A cottontail then I would be,* he thinks with an inner giggle.

His fingers tingle with the anticipated pleasure of touching the baby lyre's strings for the first time. If he needed one, that is his confirmation to play. He sits down and opens his arms in a ritual he has become used to, and in a lilac flash, the baby lyre lands on his lap.

Astor starts playing. Straightaway, the music takes on a very grave tone with deep wailing notes. The somber tone alarms everyone, including Astor.

A whisper of the baby lyre reaches Astor's mind. *Be aware—this is an exorcism, at the heart of the illness.* This immediately reassures Astor. Yet, he shudders at the word "exorcism," and senses darkness closing in around him. Concerned, he wonders if he should stop playing.

"Have no fear, Master," says the baby lyre comfortingly. "I may be young, but I've inherited all the skills and wisdom of my mother, the Lyre of Cosmic Enchantment."

Reassured, Astor glances at the ground just in time to see a dirty-white froth foaming from Newtia's mouth. At that moment a wailing note jumps higher and Newtia, further tormented in his own agony, coughs up a dark, greenish-brown mass that lands at Astor's feet.

Instantly that mass morphs into the Witch of the Dark and Fetid Waters and disappears with a high-pitched screech.

Newtia comes out of his seizure.

The music changes to a more soothing melody and then becomes a lively tune for its conclusion.

The last note is still rolling away in the Hall of the Rainbow Throne when Newtia stands up, completely recovered. Against his now-lustrous olive-green skin, his dull reddish spots have turned radiant orange.

For a brief instant, mouth agape, Newtia looks stunned. Then he scoots forward as fast as he can, his tiny claws raking against the stone floor of the throne room.

He throws himself at the feet of Lady Irena and begins speaking in a ghostly tone. "Your Highness, I need to tell you that your illness was due to a dose of poison I administered you!" he confesses.

All those around are stunned, unable to fully comprehend what was uttered.

"What are you saying?" asks Lady Irena, still recovering from her shock.

"For the promise of a companion, I inadvertently did the ugly bidding of Madame Malevolence, the Witch of the Dark and Fetid Waters, your sworn enemy."

Lord Iridio listens to Newtia, his rainbow colors waxing and waning as his anger rises. Never has the gathered group seen him in that state. Everyone remains immobile and silent. Not out of fear but out respect for a beloved leader and out of grief for an esteemed colleague.

"How could you *do* that? Not only you betrayed Lady Irena, the council and myself, but you also imperiled the harmony of the world," says Lord Iridio finally. His anger explodes into a stormy rainbow of tormented colors that could only be described as a painting from the palette of a wild-eyed artist.

Lord Iridio dislikes imprisoning anyone, especially Newtia, one of his trusted advisors. In this case, however, he has no choice. "Take him to the dungeon where he will await trial by his peers," he orders. Unseen until that order, two burly German shepherds in black-and-white uniforms appear and drag the downcast Newtia away.

A heavy silence still floats around the group, threatening to sink the joyous mood of the day. No one is more affected than the twins, Hooty-Tooty and Tooty-Hooty, who adore "Uncle Newt," as they call Newtia. They can't make sense of his actions.

It seems so unlike the Uncle Newt they love and admire.

Rewarding Astor

Once the decision to send Newtia to the dungeon is made, Lord Iridio shakes off his anger and quickly regains his naturally affable personality; the rainbow returns to its dazzling state of colors. Lord Iridio then addresses his councilors. "We gather here to honor our hero Astor for healing our beloved Lady Irena, thus saving the world from chaos. How shall we reward him?"

"Maybe we should make him a member of the Council of Overflowing Kindness," offers Mantra.

"Or a knight? A knight in shining armor. That's so romantic," suggests Miss Tortuguita, fluttering her eyelashes, green-mascaraed this time for celebration.

Astor makes a face. He starts thinking what the honor of knighthood might entail. First of all, he would need to store the armor. His room, where he keeps his belongings and games, is already crammed. Then, he would have to oil and polish the armor. That would take a lot of time and might cut into his schoolwork, home chores, and play time. Finally, although his schoolmates might envy him, his mother wouldn't like him clinking around in armor at home, much less at school.

"*Nah!*" he thinks to himself.

"He will need a horse too!" says Cri-Cri with a wink. "I have one."

"You mean your favorite rocking horse, the one you found in the arroyo dying from not being ridden?" says Talmock.

"Not that one!" says Cri-Cri, turning bright red. He doesn't want people to know he rides a wooden horse at home. "The one in my...my backyard," he stammers.

"Didn't that horse belong to a circus? Doesn't it still act like it is on parade once a day?"

"That's a horse for Don Quixote, not our hero Astor. Shame on you, Cri-Cri!" says Miss Mariposa, unfurling part of her proboscis. She came to love the way children stick their tongue out in displeasure.

All burst into a roar of laughter. The image of Cri-Cri's retired circus horse is tenderly amusing.

Astor enjoys the verbal jousting between the two friends for he understands it is born of good-natured affection.

The twins, standing next to their mother, listen with one ear each because their other ear is entirely concentrated on a low-voice discussion between them.

In the spirit of their twinness, they each raise a wing at the same time.

"Ah, my favorite twins," says Lady Irena. "What's your opinion?" She knows that the twins have inherited considerable intelligence from their parents.

"Astor could be made an earl," says Hooty-Tooty.

"Master of the Lilac Lyre," adds Tooty-Hooty, naming the new lyre.

"Earl Astor, Master of the Lilac Lyre. That sounds appropriate," muses Lady Irena aloud.

"Yes, that sounds very nice," echoes Miss Mariposa.

"I would say it's fabulous," concurs Señora Tortuga.

Lady Irena turns to Lord Iridio. "What do you think, your Lordship?"

"Let's ask Astor's opinion first," he says.

"Me, an earl?" asks Astor.

Events are moving fast, yet he is able to follow the discussion much better than he would have a month earlier.

"Do you like it?" asks Blanca.

Astor looks at her trustingly, purses his lips, and stands there lost in thought for a brief moment. "Will I have to wear armor?" he finally asks.

"No! I promise you. You won't have to wear armor," answers Lord Iridio in a reassuring voice. He understands that the idea of wearing armor is problematic for Astor.

"I like it then," says Astor.

He reaches that conclusion because he remembers that Robin Hood, one of his favorite heroes, was appointed Earl of Locksley before he became an outlaw fighting the evil Sheriff of Nottingham.

"Then it's settled," says Lord Iridio. "We are going to do it the way humans did it in the bygone times of chivalry, but with a variation of our own."

Lord Iridio raises a hand, instantly triggering a triumphant trumpet call.

Master Circonius, the Deputy Chief of Protocol, arrives bearing a ruby-red cushion on which rest a magnificent peacock feather dwarfing a ring with a gleaming green stone, and a tiny hummingbird's feather.

Following Master Circonius is a squirrel in a brown military cap and an orange-and-green uniform, who carries a crimson-red cushion;

he promptly lays it at the feet of Lord Iridio and moves out of sight, while Master Circonius stands by Lord Iridio.

"Astor, please come forward," invites Lord Iridio with an extended hand.

Gently prodded by Blanca, Astor comes to stand before Lord Iridio.

"Astor, please kneel," says Lord Iridio, pointing to the cushion.

As Astor kneels, Lord Iridio picks up the peacock feather and with it gives Astor's right shoulder a gentle tap.

Another trumpet call sounds equally triumphant.

"Arise, Sir Astor, Master of the Lilac Lyre and Earl of the Arroyo Breeze. As such, you are hereby entitled, as a Member Emeritus, to sit on the Council of Overflowing Kindness."

Lord Iridio picks up the hummingbird feather and says, "Since, like you, we do not believe in weapons, we bestow on you this hummingbird feather as a symbol of your new powers." Lord Iridio leans forward. "Young Sir Astor, a word of caution, if I may. Because your healing powers are extraordinary, this tiny feather will help you retain them. This delicate feather also will keep you humble. Do not let the power of your gift go to your head. You will lose this gift by boasting, unkindness or by misuse."

The hummingbird feather fills Astor with proud joy. He has always been awed by the power of the tiny *colibrís*, as a Mexican friend calls them in his own language.

Finally, Lord Iridio picks up the ring, the last piece on the ruby-red cushion held by Master Circonius. "Here is a ring with a green emerald. When you wear it, you will continue to see and understand all who dwell in the Kingdom of the Arroyo, just as Blanca's magic helped you do. Also, from now on, every member of the kingdom is your friend. None will harm you. Everyone will offer any assistance you may need and will come to your rescue when necessary."

As Lord Iridio has not made such a speech since Lady Irena fell ill, he pauses to catch his breath. The distinguished assembly around him erupts into applause.

Astor cherishes the wave of approval that flows over him.

"Now, Sir Astor, do you have any wishes?" asks Lord Iridio after the applause recede.

Astor is about to say no, when the Lilac Lyre speaks into his heart.

"Yes, I would like you to pardon Newtia. I believe he was deceived and manipulated by the witch."

Lord Iridio remains silent for a moment, and then gives an order. Promptly, the two guards who earlier took Newtia away now bring him back.

Returning to the brightly lit throne room from the dark dungeon, Newtia keeps blinking his eyes. He doesn't understand why he has been brought back so soon. He expected to spend longer in the dungeon, until his appearance before his peers on the Council of Overflowing Kindness.

Before Lord Iridio he stands, head hung in shame. Lord Iridio gazes a long time at Newtia's pitifully hunched body. When Lord Iridio finally speaks, he challenges Newtia with his own words. "You said to Lady Irena, 'For the promise of a companion, I inadvertently did the ugly bidding of Madame Malevolence, the Witch of the Dark and Fetid Waters, your sworn enemy.' Explain exactly what you meant."

"Your Lordship," says Newtia, raising his head to meet his sovereign's eyes. "Thank you for giving me a chance to explain my vile actions."

He hesitates before going on.

"I was fighting a great depression born of desperate loneliness. I kept that secret for fear of being ostracized. I know the fear was unfounded because you, Lady Irena, and the council would have done for me all that was possible to help me. But the combination of fear and shame, two powerfully destructive emotions, were too much for me. I hid it all from everyone."

He stops and sighs.

"One day, I assumed my human appearance and went for a walk along the arroyo. There, I encountered a woman walking her dog on a leash. 'Good morning, Madam!' I said."

Instantly the fleeting image of a man, woman, and dog that Astor saw earlier reappears in his mind. *That's what it was. I was not crazy!* he says under his breath, now able to make sense of that image.

"'Good morning to you too, Sir!' she said. 'Would you be kind enough to enlighten me about this beautiful area? This is my first visit here since I arrived from the East Coast.'"

"I was happy to share my experience of our magical place. 'This is called the Arroyo, a pristine area of unusual flora and fauna,' I began. For a while we walked and talked. Well, mostly *I* talked, giving the woman plenty of advice about visiting the arroyo. When I finished, she said, 'Thank you, sir, for your good information' and bade me good-bye.'"

He stops, his eyes looking into the past.

"We had barely taken few steps in opposite directions when I heard her say, 'You are fighting depression. I can help you. I am a certified therapist.'" I turned around, surprised that just in the span of our brief conversation, this woman had diagnosed my depression. We met the next day at a table in front of the Aquatic Center.

The woman introduced herself as Dr. MendBind and explained she had a degree from a German university. She told me that she had over twenty years of successful practice. She then took my pulse."

Newtia stops again, aware of the thick silence in the room.

"'Look me in the eye,' she said. 'Your ongoing depression is due to loneliness.'

Then Dr. MendBind pulled from her purse a vial of a potion with a smell totally alien to me. She gave me a sip, saying it would help control my depression until the cause—that is, my loneliness—could be remedied.

"As soon as I took the sip, I felt a wild urge to listen to her voice, which then sounded so enchanting. She took both my hands and looked into my eyes, saying, 'You will marry the first woman you encounter, if she is single. However, if she is married, you must kill her.' Then she repeated, 'You will kill her, if she is married. Do you understand? That is the only way to rid yourself of this curse of loneliness. You must not hesitate to kill her or you will never, *never* have another chance of healing yourself.'

"Dr. MendBind concluded our consultation by writing me a prescription. Then she gave me a large bottle of water and instructed me to drink one small glass before sunrise and another right after sunset, or, she warned, my own death would occur."

At this point in his story, Newtia stops. He looks lonelier than ever.

"Is that why you left our meetings every day at sunset, no matter what was being discussed?" asks Mantra.

Newtia nods and sighs deeply.

"Fate had it that the first woman I encountered was Lady Irena, on her way to visit her favorite fish, the cute little darters in the creek. Since I was in an altered state, I did not immediately recognize her. But I fell in love at once."

Newtia stops, looking miserable for what he is about to say.

"To my extreme distress, even when I realized who she was, I also felt an overwhelming impulse to kill her.

But a voice in my head said, *Control yourself. You need to kill her slowly to rid yourself of the curse of depression. You have access to all kinds of poisons, and you will prepare a potion for a slow death.* I did just that. I concocted a poisonous potion that I administered to Lady Irena once a week."

"How did you manage to do that?" asks Lady Irena. "You never gave me a shot!"

"That wasn't necessary. The poison was absorbed through your skin. Since I immunized myself against it, I only needed to shake hands with you. That simple contact was sufficient to transfer the poison from my hand to yours."

"You never understood the horror of your actions, huh?" interjects Señora Tortuga.

"No, not until I spat out the spell just a while ago!" Newtia confirms honestly.

Silent until then, Dame Hoota-Tooha intervenes. "If I may, I believe the explanation is rather simple."

Lord Iridio and Lady Irena simultaneously nod for her to continue.

Dame Hoota-Tooha speaks slowly and distinctly. "By choosing the name Dr. MendBind, the witch gave away everything. The simple transposition of two letters makes her name to be Dr. BendMind. I believe that the potion she administered to Newtia at their second meeting cast a spell on him. Also it really bent Newtia's mind completely to her own. The daily drinks of water she prescribed were only meant to keep the spell active and powerful. Those drinks had to be taken when the sun was not present, in times of darkness. That was the most ingenious way for Madame Malevolence, the Witch of the Dark and Fetid Waters, to make Newtia drink the dark waters she controls."

A Royal Act

"Obviously Newtia was not in his right mind," says Lord Iridio, nodding his head in understanding. "And we know that when he is not under an evil spell, he has a bright mind, full of ideas, and a heart full of compassion as well. I move that Lord Iridio pardon Newtia," says Lady Irena.

"I second that!" exclaims Cri-Cri, lifting high his now useless cane and touching his tam-o'-shanter.

"I co-second," adds Talmock, not to be outdone by his friendly rival.

"Those in favor…"

Before Lord Iridio can finish his sentence, all clamor a sonorous "Yes!"

"Those against?"

No one moves. No wing flutters, no antenna stirs in response.

All are quiet.

In his most official voice, Lord Iridio decrees, "Then a total pardon is hereby granted to Newtia, who is also restored to each and all of his official capacities."

The twins swiftly reach Newtia and embrace him. "We are so happy for you, Uncle Newt! We didn't believe for one second, make it one nanosecond, that you could poison Lady Irena…had you not been under a spell."

"Thank you, my boys, for your trust!" says Newtia, deeply moved by the royal court's vote of confidence and the owlets' love.

After a brief conversation with his wife Dame Hoota-Tooha, Professor Hoot-Hooty coughs to get the group's attention, "If it pleases your Lord and Ladyship, we would like to adopt Newtia into our family. His loneliness would be a thing of the past and I am convinced that a worthy companion would not be hard to find now that we are aware of it. As an uncle, he will be invaluable in helping raise the twins. They will benefit from his enormous knowledge and considerate spirit while Dame Hoota-Tooha and I would get welcome assistance and respite."

He looks at Newtia and adds, "Provided Newtia has no objection, of course!"

Newtia raises his eyes to the sky and a torrent of tears rolls down his cheeks.

The twins embrace each other jumping with joy.

"So it is!" decrees Lord Iridio.

❧

When Blanca and Astor return to the grassy area near the Aquatic Center, his mother is still engrossed in her reading.

She comes out of her suspended state upon Blanca's disappearing and says, "How are you doing, Astor?"

"Just fine, Mom!" he answers.

Under his breath, he adds, "If I told you the truth, you would be unhappy with me because you would think I was making up stories."

"What are you muttering?" asks his mother.

"Nothing, Mom. Just trying out a song."

Shortly afterward, they head home. On Astor's index finger is a ring with a green emerald, and hanging from his neck is a lyre. Both are invisible to his mother, or anyone else.

Heal Thy Community, Heal Thyself

The next morning Astor wakes up earlier than usual.

Shuffling his way to the breakfast table, he hears a soft buzz, which then stops. He hears it four or five times more.

Astor lets it be without any trace of irritation or dissatisfaction.

As his father hoped he would, he is starting to discover that "answers often come at their own time."

In the doorway to the kitchen, Astor stops, transfixed: his mother is already there by the stove, fixing their favorite breakfast—blueberry pancakes—while humming a lively tune.

In the six months since his father's death, Astor can't remember a workday when his mother isn't in a hurry. Sometimes mechanically but more often nervously, she is gathering herself and getting ready to leave the house.

This morning, however, Astor's mother is relaxed and cheerful.

"Good morning, Astor," she says, alerted to his presence by maternal instincts and his hesitant, shuffling walk.

"Good morning, Mom," responds Astor, puzzled but delighted.

With a theatrical gesture, his mom invites him to sit. When people want to tell something too complicated or unbelievable to their family or friends, they often start speaking immediately, frequently without much transition. It seems they are actually trying to convince themselves.

So does Astor's mother, saying, "Since I woke up, I had only one thought on my mind—how to explain my new attitude and behavior to you!"

Still, she hesitates, mindful of her story and the effect it may have on Astor.

"Yesterday, at the park near the Aquatic Center, I was reading my journal, when suddenly a tune arose in my mind. It was totally unknown to me, almost foreign in its musicality, yet real and enchanting. It felt like a serenade composed and performed for me."

She hums the tune, and instantly Astor recognizes the one he played for Lady Irena's healing.

"The fog that blurred my perception and made our lives miserable for so long just lifted. Poof! It vanished under the power of that music—like a miraculous remedy." She sighs happily and adds, "I forgot to say, I took the day off to drive you to the dentist."

Despite his distaste at the thought of having the dentist prod and poke inside his mouth, Astor can't prevent a large smile from lighting up his face.

"You're smiling," says his mother.

"Yes, I'm smiling because a remedy would do us a lot of good."

"Well, I truly feel refreshed today!" she says.

Astor keeps looking at her, pleased at his mother's apparent progress.

In a softer voice, she says, "I know now I can be the good mother that you deserve."

"You *are* a good mother.

"Do you think so?"

"Yes, I do, Mom."

Astor is convinced the music he played for Lady Irena is also helping heal his mother. Yet at no time does he connect it to his unselfish quest to heal Lady Irena and save the world from chaos.

If depression is…treatable to a large degree, there is hope for many people, thinks his mother .

Emotions and intelligence work together, like two sides of the same coin. Repeating these doctor's words to herself, Astor's mother is now confident her son is moving through his own healing process. She commits herself to fully supporting it.

Though this responsibility assigned to me at this time is a natural one, it is nonetheless a noble mission, my noble mission as a mother, she tells herself.

In a state of elation, a big smile lights her face.

It keeps evolving until her face blossoms into a radiant rosy-pink moon.

Astor also senses healing taking place in him as well.

His instinct alerts him to its long process.

A detached calm envelops him demonstrating the growth he experienced since the day he met Blanca in the arroyo. And at that moment, he experiences warmth in his heart and feels it traveling to his head.

An urge to hug his mother overtakes him. He embraces her warmly, and for the first time, kisses her on both cheeks, the Greek way.

Made in the USA
Charleston, SC
13 October 2014